The Fever

MARILYN KAYE

BANTAM BOOKS
NEW YORK • TORONTO • LONDON • SYDNEY • AUCKLAND

RL 5.5, 008–012
THE FEVER
A Bantam Skylark Book/January 2000

ISBN 0-553-48693-4

Visit us on the Web! www.randomhouse.com/kids

Published simultaneously in the United States and Canada.

PRINTED IN THE UNITED STATES OF AMERICA

OPM   10   9   8   7   6   5   4   3   2   1

Pour Louisette Fratoni et tout le monde au Café Hall 1900,

mon bureau à Paris

The Fever

one

The audience was getting restless.

Amy Candler didn't need to use any of her super-powers to know this. Any ordinary human being could hear the scraping of the folding chairs on the gymnasium floor and the rustling of people fidgeting in their seats. Not to mention the sighs of impatience as the man standing at the microphone went on and on in a monotonous voice. From where Amy was sitting with her mother, Eric, and Tasha, she could see that several members of the audience had closed their eyes. One of them was even snoring.

Amy looked sideways and caught Eric's eye. He offered

a shrug that said something like "I know, this is a pain. I'm so bored I could lie down and die."

Amy nodded. She agreed wholeheartedly. At that moment their principal, Dr. Noble, was responding to the man at the microphone with the same answer she'd given a zillion other parents.

"You may be assured that we will not allow the problems experienced by the Deep Valley or Plainview schools to occur here at Parkside."

Another parent had taken the man's place at the microphone. "But how are you going to prevent it?" the woman demanded. "Both Deep Valley and Plainview serve the same type of suburban community as Parkside. How are we going to stop these drug dealers from infiltrating our children's school? The police haven't even been able to identify how the students are coming into contact with the drugs!"

Dr. Noble's normally commanding voice had become tired. She'd been answering questions like this for almost two hours. "We will be watching our students very closely. Any change in behavior will be noticed and brought to my attention immediately."

This response didn't satisfy the woman. "But by the time their behavior changes, it's too late! They're already addicted!"

A chorus of comments created a buzz throughout

the gym. Amy sank back in her seat and looked at her mother. Nancy Candler seemed concerned too, but not as frightened as some parents. Amy knew that was because her mother trusted her and her two best friends, Eric and Tasha, to stay away from drugs.

This special parent-teacher-student meeting had been called at Parkside in response to certain highly publicized events at other suburban Los Angeles middle schools. There had been a sudden and unexpected increase in the number of students showing signs of drug abuse and addiction. Parents and teachers had a right to be concerned, and so did the students. No one Amy knew wanted to see drug dealers spreading their garbage in their middle school.

But absolutely nothing had been said at this meeting that everyone hadn't heard before. And no one had proposed any new method to keep young teens safe from drugs.

Another mother was at the microphone now. "I'll tell you why kids get into drugs. They're bored! They have nothing to do but watch TV. They have nowhere to go except for the malls. That's where the drug dealers find them, hanging out at the malls."

Amy and Tasha exchanged looks and shook their heads. Both of them went to their local mall frequently, and neither had ever been approached by a drug dealer.

The mother was still talking. "Our kids need more positive recreational experiences, more organized after-school activities. What can you do about that?"

"Very little, I'm afraid," Dr. Noble replied. "We don't have a large budget for after-school activities."

Now Amy was aware of her own mother beginning to fidget and look at her watch. There was company coming for dinner, and Nancy still had lots to do at home.

No one complained when Dr. Noble adjourned the meeting. Amy, her friends, and her mother joined the rush to the door.

Nancy was mumbling as she started the car. "It's going to take me at least an hour to get dinner on the table."

"What's for dinner?" Eric asked from the backseat.

"Eric!" Tasha chided her brother. "That's so rude!"

But Amy's mother just laughed. "Eric's just making himself feel at home," she said. "And that's what I hope you'll do too, Tasha. After all, you guys are going to be with us for two weeks."

"Two weeks," Eric mused. "What are my parents going to do in New York for two weeks without us?"

"They're on their second honeymoon, stupid," Tasha replied. "I'm sure they'll find plenty to keep them occupied."

In the front seat, Amy turned around and grinned. Personally, she was pleased that the Morgans had decided to take a vacation without their kids. It meant she would have her boyfriend and best friend staying with her in her house for two weeks.

"Who's the man coming to dinner, Mom?" she asked. "Someone *interesting*?" As the daughter of a single mother, Amy was curious about any man who came into their home.

"Not in the way you're thinking," Nancy said with a smile. "David and I are just friends, *old* friends. I must admit, I'm looking forward to seeing him. It's been a long time."

"How long?" Amy asked.

"Twelve years. David was one of my colleagues when I was working on Project Crescent."

Amy nodded. "So he was there when I was . . ." She let her voice drift off. She couldn't exactly say *born*. When you were one of twelve identical clones created in a genetic experiment, the right word didn't come to mind immediately.

"We were pretty good buddies back then," Nancy said.

"How come you haven't seen him in twelve years?" Tasha asked.

Nancy hesitated. She never liked talking about

Project Crescent, even though she knew that Amy had told Tasha and Eric all about it. Amy answered Tasha for her.

"The scientists wanted everyone to think the project had been terminated and all the clones destroyed. They were afraid that the powerful guys might become suspicious if any of the scientists got together again." She turned back to her mother. "What's he like, this David person?"

"David Hopkins," Nancy corrected her. "*Dr.* David Hopkins. Well, like I said, it's been a while since I've seen him. Back then, he was on the fast track in genetic research. He was only twenty-eight, but he'd already been published in major science and medical journals. He wrote about chromosomal duplication and tissue analysis."

This was not what Amy wanted to know. "What's he *like*?"

"He was pretty intense," her mother said. "Very driven and ambitious." She smiled. "He always looked like he needed a haircut and a shave. And I don't think he ever slept. There were heavy dark circles under his eyes, his clothes were always wrinkled, and his socks never matched. We used to tease him about that. He was pale, and he never seemed to eat. But that was twelve years ago. I don't know what he's like now."

Clearly, Dr. David Hopkins had gone through some changes. The man who appeared at the Candler home that evening didn't look at all the way Amy's mother had described him. He was muscular and tanned and looked very healthy. He was neatly groomed and casually dressed in pressed khakis and a light blue shirt. And his socks matched.

Nancy was very surprised. "David! What—What happened to you?"

His laugh was warm and easy. "It's a long story," he said. He looked past Nancy at Amy. "Is this who I think it is?"

"*She,* not it," Nancy corrected him. "Yes, David, this is Amy."

Dr. Hopkins gazed at Amy in awe. "Number Seven," he murmured.

"Well, we just call her Amy," Nancy said. "Amy, this is Dr. David Hopkins."

"Just call me Dave," he said. He echoed this when he was introduced to Tasha and Eric. And in the next few moments of conversation, Amy could see that he wasn't driven or intense anymore. He appeared to be a typical easygoing, down-to-earth southern California kind of guy.

Over a dinner of spaghetti with clam sauce, salad, and garlic bread, Dr. Hopkins explained his metamorphosis from manic scientist to laid-back family doctor.

"I got off the fast track," he told them. "After Crescent, I took on a few research projects, but nothing was quite as interesting. And I decided that I wanted a life beyond science. So, about five years ago, I moved out here to the West Coast and set up a small-town general practice, less than forty minutes from Parkside."

"How did you know I was here?" Nancy asked him.

"About a month ago, I ran into Mary Jaleski at the L.A. airport," he said. "She told me."

"Jaleski," Eric repeated. "Isn't that—?"

Amy nodded. "Mary's father was the director of Project Crescent."

Dr. Hopkins turned to Amy. "Mary told me you met James Jaleski."

Amy nodded. It was still hard to talk about Dr. Jaleski. It hadn't been that long since he died. "Tell me about Project Crescent," she urged Dr. Hopkins.

"I'm sure your mother has told you all about it," he said.

"But she's my *mother*," Amy said. "It would be nice to get an objective point of view."

Nancy pretended to be offended. "Are you suggesting that I could lie to my own daughter?"

Amy grinned. "No, but you might have exaggerated when you said I was perfect."

Dr. Hopkins looked at Tasha and Eric a little nervously. "It's okay," Amy assured him. "They're my best friends. They know everything."

He nodded, but he still looked concerned. "You have to be careful, Amy."

"I know," she assured him. She'd had too many scary experiences to even think about revealing her secret to anyone else.

So Dr. Hopkins told the story. Amy had heard it before, but it was still amazing.

"We were brought together by a government agency—scientists, geneticists, biologists, medical doctors . . . we thought we were doing something that would benefit humanity. We thought that by experimenting with DNA and cloning combined chromosomes, we would learn how to prevent terrible genetic disorders from occurring in infants."

"Only that wasn't what it was all about," Nancy said softly.

The doctor nodded. "Then James learned the truth. This so-called agency didn't care about disabled or sick children. They were an organization hiding under an official government title, and their real aim was to create a master race. They wanted to make a population of genetically superior infants who could grow up and reproduce an entire race of humans with perfect physical and mental capabilities. And with this perfect race, they could take over the world."

Amy was aware of her friends looking at her, and she blushed. She always found it a little embarrassing to be referred to as perfect.

"So that's why we shipped the clones to adoption agencies all over the world," Dr. Hopkins continued. "We blew up the laboratory and hoped that the organization would believe that all the research and the clones had been destroyed." He gazed at Amy intently. "You're the first one I've ever seen."

Amy squirmed self-consciously in her chair. "Uh, Mom, should I get the strawberries?"

"I'll get them," Nancy said, and left the table.

Dr. Hopkins smiled at Amy. "I know this must make you uncomfortable, but I have to ask. Have you ever been sick? Did you have measles, chicken pox, any of those childhood illnesses? Did you ever get the flu?"

"No," Amy replied honestly. "I've never even had a cold."

Tasha piped up. "Even when Amy falls and gets bruised, or if she cuts herself, it heals like that." She snapped her fingers.

"Amy's stronger than I am," Eric told the doctor. "A *lot* stronger. She can see and hear better than anyone."

"She can memorize ten irregular French verbs in five minutes," Tasha reported. "And she can do algebra problems in her head."

Now Amy was getting seriously embarrassed. "Guys, cut it out!"

"But it's true, Amy," Tasha insisted.

Amy couldn't deny that. "Could we please stop talking about me?"

Nancy returned with the strawberries and whipped cream. "Tell us about the work you're doing now, David."

"I'm a small-town doctor," he said. "I even make house calls! I deal with ordinary, everyday injuries and illnesses. If I suspect that a patient has a serious problem, I send that patient on to a specialist. On an average day, I'll give a tetanus shot to someone who stepped on a nail, set a broken arm, check out a couple of sore throats, stitch up a cut, pierce some ears . . ."

Both Amy and Tasha perked up at that bit of news. "What did you say?" they asked in unison.

"About stitches?"

"No," Amy said, "after that!"

Nancy shook her head wearily. "The girls want to get their ears pierced, David. They've been talking about it for ages."

"Well, they're the right age," Dr. Hopkins said. "The

girls who show up in my office are around twelve. Of course, I also get the older ones, who want noses and tongues and eyebrows pierced. Boys *and* girls."

"Gross," Eric commented.

"My parents gave me permission," Tasha said. "As long as I have it done by a real doctor and not at a jewelry store. Only, I have to pay for it myself."

"Don't complain about that," Amy said. "*I* can't even get permission for piercing."

Nancy frowned. "It's just that I wouldn't want Amy to have it done at a store either. But I don't want her to get near a doctor."

Dr. Hopkins nodded. "I understand. It's not safe for you to be seen by a medical doctor, Amy. A simple blood test could reveal to them some very unusual information about you."

"All doctors aren't evil," Amy protested. "They might not want to hurt me, you know."

"Of course not," Dr. Hopkins said. "But if they detect something special about you, they're bound to be intrigued by the information. And we don't want anyone getting too interested in you, do we?"

Amy's ears picked up on the *we*. As if he was a part of her life. Well, since he'd been on the Project Crescent team, maybe in a way he was. And then a *very* interesting possibility occurred to her.

"But if the doctor was a personal friend," she said carefully, "someone you could trust not to tell anyone . . ."

"Amy," her mother warned.

Dr. Hopkins caught on, and he grinned. "It's up to your mother."

Amy looked at her mother anxiously. "Mom?"

Nancy sighed. "Well, if it's okay with David . . ."

"For both of us?" Tasha asked eagerly. "Please?"

Dr. Hopkins looked at her seriously. "Are you sure your parents approve?"

Tasha nodded, and Nancy confirmed it.

"How much do you charge?" Tasha asked. "I've got thirty dollars saved up."

"Well, let's see," Dr. Hopkins said seriously. His brow puckered, and he frowned, as if he was doing some major mental calculations. "How about if I tell you the cost is—free?"

It took a second for this to sink in. When it did, Amy and Tasha let out squeals of joy and gave each other a high five.

In their side-by-side twin beds that night, Amy was still enthralled by their good luck. "I can't believe it," she said. "Tomorrow at this time we'll have pierced ears!"

"Yeah," Tasha said.

"What's the matter?" Amy asked.

"Nothing."

But Amy knew better. "Oh, right, I forgot. You don't like needles."

"It's not that I don't like needles," Tasha began, but Amy finished for her.

"It's just that you're scared to death of them."

Tasha let out a little whimper. "Right."

Amy reached across the space that separated the beds and grabbed Tasha's hand. "It's okay, I'll be there. Besides, they don't use needles to pierce ears."

"But I bet it's just as bad—maybe worse," Tasha said.

"Just think about the earrings you'll be able to wear."

"Okay," Tasha whispered. "I'll be brave."

Amy gave Tasha's hand a squeeze. Then she drifted off to sleep, happily dreaming of silver hoops and tiny pearl studs.

two 2

In Amy's social studies class, the teacher always devoted the last ten minutes to current events. Since everyone was still talking about last evening's special meeting and the problems at other middle schools, today's topic was drug abuse.

"Does anyone have any thoughts on how we can keep drugs out of Parkside?" Ms. Lindsay asked.

A hand shot up—and of course it belonged to Jeanine Bryant. She always wanted to be first. And since she was the only one in the class with her hand up, Ms. Lindsay had to call on her. "Yes, Jeanine?"

Jeanine stood up. This wasn't necessary, but Jeanine liked to make sure everyone could see her.

"We have to do everything we can to keep drugs out of Parkside," she declared. "Drugs are destroying the youth of our nation! We cannot overestimate the danger this represents to our society. The epidemic of drug use among teens must be stopped."

Amy wasn't the only one in the class who rolled her eyes. It was clear that Jeanine wasn't using her own words.

"I'm sure everyone agrees with you, Jeanine," Ms. Lindsay said. "But do you have any specific ideas on how we can accomplish this?"

"Yes, I do," Jeanine replied. "All lockers should be searched every day. Students should be given lie-detector tests to find out if they've been taking drugs outside of school. And we need X-ray machines at the school entrance, like the kind they have at airports, to make sure no one's hiding any drugs in their backpacks."

"How about strip searches in homeroom?" a boy called out, and everyone started laughing.

Ms. Lindsay made a shushing sound, but she couldn't help smiling. "He's got a point, Jeanine. You're talking about taking some extreme measures."

"We have to take extreme measures," Jeanine stated

flatly. "This is *serious*. I don't want Parkside to get a reputation like Deep Valley has now. And no one should get a second chance, either. If anyone is discovered using drugs, they should be expelled from school immediately and sent to a juvenile detention center."

Amy was fed up with Jeanine's know-it-all tone. "Why not just shoot them on the spot?" she suggested sarcastically.

Jeanine gazed at Amy with an expression of exaggerated horror and disbelief. "Amy Candler! Do you approve of drug use?"

"Of course not," Amy replied. "But kids who are caught with drugs for the first time shouldn't be thrown in jail. They need help and counseling. The really bad guys are the pushers, who take advantage of kids."

Jeanine sniffed. "If you get rid of the addicts, the pushers won't have anyone to sell their drugs to. They'll go out of business."

Ms. Lindsay was always telling them not to make fun of anyone's point of view, but Jeanine was being totally illogical. "That's stupid," Amy said bluntly. "They'll just create new users. Pushers can always find kids who are unhappy or depressed. Kids who feel like they don't fit in. They're the targets for the pushers."

Jeanine's eyes had darkened. She did not like to be

called stupid. "You sound like someone who knows all about kids who don't fit in, Amy. Do you consider yourself a misfit?"

Amy had no chance to come back with a cool retort: The bell rang. But Jeanine managed to get in one more insult before Amy could walk out the door. She was on Amy's right, and she spoke in an unnecessarily loud voice.

"Amy, you've lost an earring."

Amy's hand flew to her right ear. Sure enough, one of the stick-on gems she'd put on that morning had fallen off.

"Good grief, Amy, you don't have holes in your earlobes!" Jeanine squealed. "Are you still using stick-ons? What's the matter, are you afraid of getting your ears pierced?"

Amy flushed, but she couldn't think of a decent comeback. Thank goodness tomorrow she'd be wearing real pierced earrings.

"I can't stand Jeanine Bryant," she declared to Tasha as they waited outside school for Nancy to pick them up.

"What else is new?" Tasha asked.

Amy knew what she meant. Amy and Jeanine had been enemies since first grade. Jeanine liked to be number one and resented the fact that Amy was always a little better at everything than she was. Nothing would make Jeanine happier than to find a good reason to ridicule Amy. Pierced ears weren't much, but they were something.

"Well, she can't laugh at my ears tomorrow," Amy said.

"Yeah," Tasha agreed. "Today's the big day, I guess."

Amy had briefly forgotten Tasha's fear. "Come on, Tasha, you said you'd be brave. It's not going to hurt much."

"How do you know? You've never had your ears pierced before. Anyway, you're stronger than regular people. You probably don't even feel pain."

"Sure I do," Amy said.

"As much as me?"

"I don't know, I'm not you." Amy looked at Tasha with compassion. "Listen. If you want, I'll stay with you and hold your hand."

Tasha tried to smile, but the smile quivered around the edges. "Amy . . ."

"What?"

"If I cry . . . don't tell Eric, okay?"

"Never," Amy promised. "Cross my heart." She could have sworn she saw the glimmer of tears in Tasha's eyes already. "Tasha, you're my best friend. I'd never make fun of you."

"Not even with your boyfriend?"

"Absolutely not. Tasha, you were my best friend long before Eric became my boyfriend. Best friends always come first."

Tasha managed another quivering smile, and she whispered in Amy's ear. "Thanks. I'd hug you right now if Jeanine wasn't watching us."

Amy approved. She certainly didn't want to give Jeanine any more ammunition to use against her. She spotted her mother's car turning into the parking lot and waved.

"How was your day, girls?" Nancy asked as Amy jumped into the front seat and Tasha got into the back.

"Fine," they chorused automatically. Tasha, with her usual good manners, then responded with "How was *your* day, Ms. Candler?"

"Hectic," Nancy said cheerfully. "This new position I'm in at the university is taking up a lot of time. But I'm enjoying it. Amy, could you turn on the radio?"

Amy obliged, pushing the button that would bring in her favorite station. As the car filled with the sounds of rap, Nancy groaned. "Amy, you know how I hate that stuff. I don't know how you kids can listen to it."

Amy sighed. They went through this ritual every time they were in the car together. She hit the button that would connect them with the all-news station.

Personally, Amy thought the news was a lot more depressing than any rap song. A shooting, a robbery, another drug bust . . . wasn't there ever any good news?

It was as if the announcer had read her mind. "And now for some happier events," he said. "Los Angeles real estate mogul and noted philanthropist Ace Tolliver called a news conference today to make an announcement. This is what he had to say."

A deep, strong voice spoke emotionally. "Although I have no children of my own, like everyone else, I am deeply concerned about the plight of today's youth. The recent reports of drug outbreaks among young teens in suburban communities bothers me enormously, and I want to do something about it. This morning I read a report in a community newspaper about a meeting held at Parkside Middle School yesterday. According to this article, there is a need for more positive recreational outlets for young people, places for them to go. This gave me an idea. I have decided to establish a chain of teen clubs throughout the suburban Los Angeles area."

Another voice spoke up. "Mr. Tolliver, what do you mean by a teen club? Some sort of school-related activity?"

The tycoon laughed. "No, no, nothing like that. As I recall from my own youth, anything related to the school system had a 'no fun' tag attached to it. What I'm talking about here are cool joints for kids, places where they're safe from drugs, violence, *and* grown-ups! At my clubs, kids can sit around and talk, they can dance, they can have snacks, they can hang out and be themselves without feeling they're under the scrutiny of teachers or parents."

"Are you saying there won't be any supervision?" another reporter asked.

"Of course there will be supervision. We'll have bouncers, just as they have in nightclubs and discos. They'll break up any fights and will keep the place orderly. They will also make sure that all patrons are between the ages of eleven and fifteen. I want kids to feel safe, but I also want them to feel free."

His words had the effect of making Tasha momentarily forget about the approaching ear piercing. "Wow, that sounds very cool," she said.

"Shhh," Amy said. Tolliver was still talking.

"I'm thinking about having special evenings with poetry readings, inviting local bands to play, making space on the wall to exhibit young people's artwork, providing a few computers with Internet access. A giant-screen TV for special events."

"When do you expect these clubs to open?"

"Sooner than you think. As some of you know, I'm a

take-charge, can-do kind of guy. When I took over that fleabag hotel on the south side, I had something first-class up and running in two weeks. I'll have this first club going in three days."

"Where?" someone asked.

"Since the idea came from Parkside Middle School, I'm setting up the first club, a prototype, in the Parkside community. My people have located a disco that recently went out of business in the basement of the Standard Building on Prince Street. I've got a whole workforce there right now as we speak, and I can tell you with complete confidence that we will have the grand opening of Ace's Space this Saturday night."

The regular radio announcer came back on. "So once again tycoon Ace Tolliver puts his fortune to good use. And now, on to the terrorist bombing yesterday in . . ."

But no one was listening anymore.

"I can't believe it!" Tasha squealed. "Prince Street! We can *walk* there!"

Amy was excited too. "Mom, who is this Ace Tolliver guy?"

"Some very rich man who gives a lot of money away," Nancy said.

"Can we go to the grand opening on Saturday?"

"We'll see." That was her mother's automatic response

to everything. But it usually meant yes. Amy turned around and nodded to Tasha, and Tasha grinned back. But then Tasha must have remembered where they were going, because her smile disappeared. And by the time they turned onto the street where Dr. Hopkins had his office, she was deathly pale.

Amy's mother could see her in the rearview mirror. "You know, Tasha," she said, "you don't have to do this. Many people live happy lives without ever getting their ears pierced."

"I'm not going to chicken out," Tasha declared faintly.

"Mom, are you sure this is the right address?" Amy asked as her mother parked the car in front of a house that looked more like a country cottage than a doctor's office. But then Dr. Hopkins had said his office was in a part of his home. And there he was at the door, waving and welcoming them in.

"You girls ready to get pierced?" he asked jovially. "I'm on my own since it's after office hours and my nurse went home. It should actually speed up the procedure."

Tasha let out a low moan. But her face was fixed in an expression of determination. She even insisted on going first—though she also insisted that Amy and

Nancy stay with her. Dr. Hopkins must have sensed her anxiety, because he kept up a cheerful stream of chatter, while he swabbed her earlobes with some strong-smelling stuff. Then he pulled out something that looked like a staple gun.

"Just a pinch," he murmured. "That's all you'll feel."

"Eeek!" Tasha squealed, and then "Eeek!" again as he pierced the other ear.

"Now, that wasn't so bad, was it?" he asked.

"Easy for you to say," Tasha muttered, but then she looked in the mirror. This time she squealed in delight. "Amy! Look!" Tiny gold balls gleamed in her earlobes.

"They're not real gold," Dr. Hopkins told her, "but they're made of a special nonallergenic metal, so you shouldn't have any kind of reaction to them." He was resterilizing his instrument as he spoke. "Amy, are you ready?"

"Sure," Amy said, pleased to see what the temporary earrings looked like. Jeanine would think they were real gold. She sat down on the stool and allowed Dr. Hopkins to swab her earlobes. Her mother gave her an encouraging smile. Tasha gazed at her in admiration.

"You're so fearless," Tasha said. "I swear, sometimes I think you're like Xena, the Warrior Princess."

Amy laughed. Maybe that was why she was unprepared for the sting of the ear-piercing instrument. "Ouch!" she yelped. The other ear wasn't any easier. She let out another yelp.

"All done," Dr. Hopkins said, putting a cotton pad with a small bloodstain on his desk. He handed Amy a mirror so she could admire herself.

"Did that really hurt, sweetie?" her mother asked.

Amy was embarrassed. "No, I was just surprised."

Tasha grinned. "I'll bet you yelled like that just to make me feel better about being such a wimp."

Amy nodded, but that wasn't really true. The ear piercing had produced a real burning sensation. Even so, it was worth it. Her gold balls looked just as good as Tasha's. Her ears still hurt, but she and Tasha hugged in triumph.

Dr. Hopkins lectured them on keeping their earlobes clean. "And don't be in any rush to buy yourselves new earrings, because you can't take these balls out for three weeks," he told them. "If you do, the holes will close up and you'll have to have them repierced."

"No thanks," Tasha said. "I'll keep mine in for *four* weeks."

Dr. Hopkins laughed and offered to give them a tour of the living quarters in the house.

When they returned to the office waiting room, he

pointed out a large box. "That's my new electrocardio-graph equipment," he announced proudly. "State-of-the-art."

"It looks huge," Nancy commented.

He nodded. "I can't even lift it. I'm waiting for a friend to come by and help me move it into the exam-ining room."

"I'll help you now," Amy offered.

He smiled. "That's kind of you, Amy, but it's very heavy."

Amy and her mother exchanged grins. "David," Nancy said, "have you forgotten who you're talk-ing to?"

Dr. Hopkins's eyes widened. "She's that strong? Okay, let's give it a try." He tipped the box so he could grab it by the bottom, then pulled it so that Amy could get her hands under the other side.

The box *was* heavy. Even with her unnatural strength, Amy had to exert herself. But they managed to get the box into the examining room, and Dr. Hop-kins was very impressed.

"Show me another one of your talents," he urged. Amy couldn't refuse. She looked around the office and noticed a stack of papers on his desk, way over on the other side of the room. A normal person wouldn't be able to read the papers from that distance.

" 'To the Director of Camp Sunnyside,' " she read aloud. " 'I have examined the prospective camper, Patricia Albright. I can certify that she is in excellent health and will be able to participate fully in all camp activities.' "

"Amazing!" Dr. Hopkins exclaimed.

Amy rubbed the bridge of her nose. She'd had to squint to read that letter. The print had been awfully small.

"I'd like to test your hearing," the doctor said eagerly, but Nancy intervened.

"Another time, David," she said. "I have to feed the kids and go to a lecture tonight at the university."

Amy and Tasha thanked him, and Nancy told him she'd call soon. Now that the procedure was over, the girls were in great spirits. Nancy even let them listen to a rock station on the car radio and they sang along all the way home.

Eric was just returning from basketball practice when they pulled into the driveway. Amy and Tasha eagerly showed him their ears, and Amy assured him that Tasha hadn't fainted. Nancy forbade any talk of piercing over dinner, but they told Eric about the cute house Dr. Hopkins lived in and how nice he was.

"You should have seen his face when Amy moved the huge box with him," Tasha remarked. "He was so impressed!"

"You showed him how strong you are?" Eric asked. He frowned. "I know he knows all about you, but to actually show him any of your skills seems risky."

"Normally I'd agree with you," Nancy said, "but Dr. Hopkins can be trusted."

Eric still didn't look pleased, and that gave Amy a nice warm feeling. Even though she was much stronger than he was, he felt protective of her.

It wasn't until Nancy had left for her lecture that Amy and Tasha could describe the gory procedure.

"I don't get it," Eric said. "Why do you want to put yourself through pain for earrings? It must be a girl thing."

"Not true!" Tasha retorted. "Lots of guys get pierced. Not just in the ears, either. You know Parker Davies? He's got a pierced tongue."

"Yeah, well, Parker Davies is a freak."

"Is not."

"Is so."

Amy knew she was going to have to put up with this brother-and-sister bickering until the end of the following week, but she was still relieved when Tasha announced she was going upstairs to do some homework. And Amy wasn't relieved just because she wouldn't have to listen to any more arguing that evening. It was nice being alone on the living room sofa with Eric.

"You can tell me the truth now," he said.

"The truth about what?"

"Did Tasha scream and throw a fit?"

"No, not a bit," Amy replied. "She was very brave. I was impressed, too, because it really did hurt."

"It hurt *you*? That can't be."

"Yes, it even hurt me," Amy admitted. "But don't you think they look cool?"

"They're okay," Eric said. "But I think you need prettier earrings." He reached into his jeans pocket and pulled out a little box. Amy squealed.

"What's that?"

"Open it and find out."

She did. Inside the box, nestled in a bit of cotton, were two little red enamel hearts.

"Oh, Eric." She sighed. "They're beautiful! Thank you!"

"Put them on," he urged.

Amy groaned. "I can't. Dr. Hopkins said we should wear these nonallergenic earrings he gave us for the next three weeks. But I swear, the minute three weeks are up, these little hearts are going into my ears. And they're never coming out."

Eric laughed. "Don't say that. Now that you have pierced ears, I know what I can get you for every birthday and Christmas present."

"Oh, good," Amy said happily. "Let's see . . . I want

pearls and emeralds and . . ." she was about to add "di-
amonds and rubies" when a yawn escaped her lips.

Eric pretended to be offended. "Am I boring you?"

"No way, never," Amy assured him. "I'm just sleepy."

"But it's only eight-thirty!"

"Really? It feels later. Want to watch TV?"

"Sure." Eric turned it on. "What do you want to
watch?"

"I don't care." Amy yawned again. "Whatever . . ."
She felt like she needed to give her eyes a rest.

Then Eric's voice seemed to come from far away.
"Hey, Amy!"

She opened her eyes. "Huh?"

"You fell asleep!"

"I did?" Amy was surprised. She hardly ever went to
sleep before bedtime. "I guess it was all the excitement
today," she murmured. She leaned over and gave Eric a
kiss. "Nighty-night."

She could barely make it up the stairs. It even took
effort to tell Tasha, who was finishing up her homework, good night. And then Amy was fast asleep the
second her head hit the pillow.

three

"What do you know about this teen club that's opening tonight?" Eric's friend Kyle Osborne asked him. The two boys were shooting hoops on Eric's driveway Saturday afternoon.

"It's called Ace's Space," Eric reported. "There's going to be a whole chain of them, but the one in Parkside is the first to open." He caught the ball Kyle threw at him. "Wanna go?"

"I don't know," Kyle said. "Is it going to be like one of those city youth things? My mother made me go last summer." He shuddered. "Some old hippie had us sitting around, singing folk songs while he played the guitar."

Eric knew the kind of event Kyle was talking about. He'd gone to a teen group like that at a church once. "Nah, I don't think so. I saw this guy Tolliver being interviewed on the news yesterday. He was joking around with the reporter, saying his clubs wouldn't have any educational or uplifting messages. He wants the focus to be on kids hanging out and enjoying themselves. He said he could remember being a young teen, so he knows what we like."

Kyle wasn't impressed. "Adults are always saying that. Then they try to jam some goody-goody wholesome stuff down your throat. All I can say is they must have been pretty sad teens themselves if they think we want to sit around in a circle and sing 'Michael, Row the Boat Ashore.' " He made a gagging sound. "Or something even worse, like 'Kumbaya.' " He ran under the net to grab the ball Eric had thrown and began to dribble.

"I don't think there'll be any songs like that at Ace's Space tonight," Eric said. He danced around Kyle, flapping his arms to stop him from throwing the ball. "The Punksters are going to play."

That bit of information disrupted Kyle's dribble rhythm, and Eric snatched the ball away. Whirling around, he made an easy basket.

"Are you serious?" Kyle asked. "The *Punksters*?"

"That's what Tolliver said on TV."

Eric knew this would alter Kyle's opinion of Ace's Space. The Punksters were a local band who had actually cut an album a couple of years earlier. One of the cuts had even been made into a music video. The band hadn't done much since, but they were still pretty hot in the area. Sometimes when a major rock band played a concert, the Punksters opened for them. They had a great look that incorporated shaved heads, numerous body piercings, and tattoos. Parents hated them, which was another point in their favor.

It was clear from Kyle's expression that Ace's Space had gone way up in his estimation. But now he had another concern. "What's this deal going to cost me?"

"Nothing tonight," Eric informed him. "Tolliver's picking up the whole tab for the grand opening. It's free."

"What's the catch?"

"No catch. After tonight there'll be a five-dollar cover charge, plus you pay for food and drinks."

"I knew it sounded too good to be true," Kyle grumbled. He was trying to get the ball away from Eric with no success.

Eric continued to dribble at high speed while he defended the tycoon. "Tolliver's a businessman; he's not doing it out of charity. And this is good business. He gets the kids into the place tonight, gets them hooked, and then they'll be willing to pay. Look, if it was free all the time, it would be one of those government-funded things, and they'd be hitting us with all that moral and ethical stuff."

"That's a good point," Kyle admitted. "Hey, here comes your girlfriend."

Eric turned, and Kyle took advantage of his distraction to grab the ball and attempt another basket. At least he hadn't been lying. Eric waved as Amy came toward them.

"You guys want to come over for lunch?" she asked. "Tasha and I are making grilled cheese sandwiches."

Kyle looked happy. "Can I have mine with tomato?"

Amy rolled her eyes. "This isn't a restaurant, Kyle." She snatched the ball away from him, aimed, and tossed a perfect basket.

"Excellent!" Eric crowed, but Kyle shook his head.

"Pure luck," he murmured to Eric. "She can't do it again."

"Wanna bet?" Eric asked. "A dollar says Amy pulls off another clean one."

"You're on," Kyle agreed. He collected the ball and tossed it to Amy. "Let's see you do that again."

Amy threw the ball. But this time it hit the basket rim and bounced off.

"Told ya!" Kyle yelled triumphantly.

Eric just shrugged. Kyle, of course, didn't know that Amy could always make a basket if she wanted to. With her perfect aim, perfect vision, and physical strength, she could have done it from twice the distance. But Amy often missed on purpose so that no one would get suspicious about her extraordinary skills. Eric just wished she hadn't decided to do that right then, when he had a bet going.

Kyle ran to Amy's back door while Eric stayed behind. "You cost me a dollar," he whispered to Amy as they headed in.

"I know," Amy said. "I'm sorry."

"Then why did you miss the basket?"

"I don't know. I didn't do it on purpose. I guess I'm just tired."

"You've been tired a lot lately," Eric commented.

"I haven't been sleeping too well," Amy told him as they joined Kyle and Tasha in the kitchen. "I keep waking up."

Tasha caught those words. "Are you having that dream again?" she asked with concern.

"No, not *that* dream," Amy said with a meaningful

look toward Kyle. She didn't want Tasha to say anything more about Amy's old nightmare—the one where she was enclosed in glass and surrounded by fire. It was based on an actual memory of the time she'd been rescued from the burning laboratory by her mother.

"Just some weird dreams," she went on. "I can't even remember what they're about when I wake up."

"You still want to go to the opening of Ace's Space tonight, don't you?" Eric asked anxiously.

"Absolutely," Amy promised.

As they were getting ready to leave that evening, Eric thought Amy looked better. But that might have been because she was wearing lipstick, a short skirt, and an off-the-shoulder blouse.

Nancy wasn't too thrilled with her look. "Amy, isn't that a little too, well, mature?"

"Mom, lay off! I'll wear what I want to wear, okay?"

Amy's tone was oddly sharp, and Eric looked at her in surprise. He tried to smooth things over. "Don't worry, Ms. Candler, I'll watch out for her," he declared. Everyone had a little laugh at that, since they all knew Amy was much stronger than he was.

Nancy gave them a lift to Prince Street. Normally

it was a very quiet street. That night, however, a large crowd had gathered, and trucks painted with the television station logos were parked everywhere. Tolliver himself was there to cut the ribbon.

The tycoon was speaking into a microphone, but the crowd was so noisy that Eric couldn't hear him. "What's he saying?" Eric asked Amy.

Amy frowned and her brow puckered. "Something about . . . need to trust teens . . . young adults . . . I can't get it all."

There was a big roar from the crowd when the doors of the building opened, and everyone lunged forward. Eric grabbed Amy's hand, and they allowed themselves to be moved along with the masses of people. As they entered the lobby, they encountered three husky men who were checking everyone out. When they saw kids who looked like they might be over fifteen, they stopped them and asked to see identification.

No one in Amy and Eric's group was stopped, which disappointed Eric a little—he figured it might really impress Amy if the security men thought he was sixteen. They moved on through double doors leading to a wide curved staircase. A boy band was blasting from loudspeakers as they scrambled down the stairs.

The space might have been called a basement at one time, but that certainly wasn't what it looked like now. It was vast and open, all black and white and shiny. Tables and chairs surrounded a dance floor over which an old-fashioned disco ball spun around, shooting sparks of light.

"Come on, let's get something to eat," Kyle said, and he and Tasha moved toward the circular chrome bar. Eric grabbed Amy's hand and they edged their way through the mob to get a real look around. After a complete tour of the area, Eric had formed a firm opinion about Ace's Space.

"This," he declared, "is very cool."

"It's pretty glitzy," Amy admitted.

It wasn't quite finished. A barrier kept kids from going into a space where Eric saw the phone jacks and plugs necessary for Internet connections. In another area, massive video games hadn't been completely installed. But even so, it was clear that middle-school students and young teens in general now had a very good place to hang out. There was no sign of the Punksters yet, but the music blaring across the room was nicely mixed, obviously by a professional disc jockey.

They found Tasha and Kyle, along with some other Parkside kids, at the bar, eating little hot dogs on toothpicks and drinking from glasses filled with frothy pink stuff. "What is it?" Amy asked.

"It tastes like melted raspberry sherbet," Tasha told her. "Try it."

Amy took a sip and wrinkled her nose. "Too sweet."

"You can get a regular soda," Kyle told her, but Amy shook her head.

"I'm not thirsty," she said. "Isn't that Ace Tolliver over there?"

Eric turned to look. Sure enough, the tycoon himself, with a burly guard on either side, was making his way through the crowd, stopping every now and then to shake a hand. Eric watched him in admiration. The man was probably around the same age as Eric's father, but any similarity ended there.

Ace Tolliver strode across the floor with the kind of self-assurance and confidence that Eric imagined only a self-made millionaire could have. His unlined face was tanned, he had all his hair, and he looked like a guy who worked out regularly. He wore a suit, but the jacket was open and the tie was loosened, so he still managed to seem casual.

Other people were admiring him too. Eric heard his own sister practically swooning. "For an old guy, he's really handsome. Don't you think he's handsome, Amy?"

"Huh? Who?"

"Ace Tolliver! I think he looks like the librarian guy on *Buffy*."

"He's okay."

Eric thought her voice sounded a little lackluster. "Are *you* okay?"

"Sure," Amy said. "I'm just a little tired."

"Ooh, he's coming this way," Tasha said excitedly.

Eric turned and found himself face to face with the great man himself. Tolliver smiled broadly, exposing gleaming white teeth. "Mind if I join you guys?"

"Sure," Eric said. "I mean, no, we don't mind. Hey, it's your place, you can be anywhere you want, right?"

One of the burly guys produced another bar stool, and Tolliver sat down. "I'm Ace Tolliver," he said, as if they didn't know.

Kyle was the first to recover and introduce himself. Tasha, Eric, and Amy followed suit. When they'd finished, Tolliver closed his eyes for a moment. "Okay, let me see if I've got these right. Amy Candler, Eric Morgan . . ." He repeated each of their names correctly. They were all astonished. "I took a memory course once," Tolliver explained. "It's very good for business. You make friends a lot more easily too."

He was talking as if he expected them to be his

friends. Even though this was the first time Eric had ever been around such a super-rich important person, he felt almost comfortable. "Great place you got here," he said.

"You think so?" Tolliver asked eagerly, as if Eric's opinion actually meant something to him. "I really want this joint to work. There's nothing else like it, you know. There are hangouts for older teens, sure, but nothing for you guys."

"I think you're doing something very nice for us," Tasha piped up.

Tolliver laughed warmly. "Well, just between us, I'm no do-gooder. I'm a real businessman, and I expect to turn a very tidy profit with a string of these clubs."

"There's nothing wrong with making a profit," Kyle remarked.

Tolliver agreed. "Absolutely; that's what business is all about. And as long as you can do this without exploiting anyone, you can maintain integrity and ethics and still run a profitable enterprise. I plan to keep the prices low enough for the average kid to take advantage of this place."

Eric was even more impressed. "But it must cost a lot to run a place like this. Isn't the rent very high?"

"Not really," Tolliver said. He grinned. "I'll share a

secret with you. I own the building. I'm the only land-lord I have to worry about."

They all smiled at his little joke. By now the dance floor was packed and the whole place was rocking.

"Are the Punksters really going to show up?" Kyle asked.

Tolliver nodded. "Ten minutes. You guys like the group, right? That's what I've heard. Listen, I'm think-ing about starting up a sort of advisory panel. I'm not all that in touch with what you folks are into, and I could use some help. You interested?"

He was looking directly at Eric, and Eric wasn't sure if he was speaking to all of them or only to him. In any case, Eric had no problem responding.

"Yeah, for sure, no problem!"

"I might even be able to come up with a stipend for the panel," Tolliver mused. "To pay for your time." He pulled a little pad and a tiny gold pen from his jacket pocket. "Eric Morgan, right?" he said, writing Eric's name down. "What's your phone number?"

Eric was dazzled. This was phenomenal. He gladly gave the tycoon his number. "Say, how do you remem-ber names so well?" he asked.

"There's a trick," Tolliver told him. "You associate the face with a word that can remind you of the name. Like . . . Amy Candler here. She looks bright, and a candle is bright. Candle, Candler, you see? She looks friendly, and the word for friend in French is *ami.* Get it?"

Personally, at that very minute, Eric didn't think Amy looked all that friendly. She was staring at Tolliver without even smiling.

"I'll be in touch," Ace Tolliver said to Eric. His two bodyguards magically appeared by his side, and he strode off.

"That guy is so unbelievably cool!" Eric said. He turned to Amy. "Don't you think so?"

Amy shrugged. "I think he's creepy."

The other three stared at her in utter bewilderment. "Why?" Tasha asked.

Amy rubbed her forehead and grimaced. "I don't know," she said vaguely. Then she said, "It's hot in here."

It was then that Eric realized she was sweating. He had never seen Amy sweat before. "You want to go outside and get some fresh air?"

Amy mumbled something.

"What did you say?" Eric asked.

"I want to go home."

Kyle was dismayed. "Now? But the Punksters are going to play!"

"I want to go home," Amy repeated.

Now Eric was alarmed. Maybe it was just the strobe lights in the club, but he thought she looked pale. "We'll go call your mother to come get us."

"You guys can stay," Amy murmured, but by now Tasha had her by one hand and Eric was holding the other. They led her toward the stairs. Kyle stayed behind.

In the building's lobby, Eric found a bank of pay phones and called Amy's mother.

"Ms. Candler? It's Eric. Amy's not feeling well. She wants to come home."

"What?"

Eric wasn't surprised that Nancy sounded more upset than the average mother would. Amy was never sick. It seemed like only seconds later that Nancy pulled up in front of the building.

In the car Amy leaned against the window and didn't speak. Nancy kept taking her eyes off the road to look at her worriedly. In the backseat, Tasha and Eric were silent.

But in the five minutes it took them to get home, Amy revived. And when they got out of the car, she looked like her normal self. "I'm okay now," she assured them, walking to the house on her own.

Nancy wasn't satisfied. Once inside the house, she

made Amy lie down on the sofa while she called Dr. Hopkins.

"This is so silly," Amy complained to Eric and Tasha. "I don't need to lie down. I'm fine."

"You weren't fine in the club," Eric said.

"It was just too hot," Amy said. "I feel hot and cold like other people, you know."

But Eric hadn't thought it was hot at all in the club.

A few moments later Nancy reappeared in the living room. "David says it could have been something you ate or drank."

"I only had a little sip of that pink stuff," Amy said. "Maybe there was something in it."

"Like what?" Nancy asked.

"I don't know," Amy said. "Something alcoholic?"

"No way," Eric objected. "Ace Tolliver wouldn't allow any alcohol in that place. The whole point is to make it safe for kids."

"Besides," Tasha added, "I drank two of those raspberry things and I feel fine."

"Maybe you're allergic to raspberries," Eric said.

Amy shook her head. "I'm not allergic to anything. And like I said, I'm okay now." She yawned. "Just tired."

"Then go to bed," Nancy said, the worry lines still creasing her forehead.

"Okay," Amy said agreeably. " 'Night, everyone." She walked across the living room to the stairs and climbed them rapidly. Eric thought she seemed perfectly normal.

But even so, he could see worry lines on Tasha's forehead too. And he could feel them on his own.

four

After her morning shower on Monday, Tasha returned to Amy's bedroom. She was surprised to see that Amy was still in bed, especially since she was clearly awake. Her eyes were wide open, and she was staring at the ceiling with a peculiar intensity.

Tasha followed her friend's eyes with her own. She didn't see anything particularly interesting on the ceiling, but of course that didn't mean Amy couldn't see something.

"What are you looking at?" she asked.

"There used to be some spots on the ceiling," Amy

said. "A little cluster of spots, from back when the roof leaked when I was little. They aren't there anymore."

Tasha couldn't understand why Amy would find that interesting. "Maybe they faded," she said. Then she noticed shadows under Amy's eyes. "Didn't you sleep well last night?"

"I kept having dreams. Nothing I can remember. Just a lingering feeling."

"What kind of feeling?"

"Like . . . Like I'm invisible! No, not really invisible, just sort of . . . not there."

"I have some pretty wild dreams sometimes too," Tasha said comfortingly. "Once I dreamed that I walked into a class at school and everyone stared at me. Then I realized I didn't have any clothes on! What do you think that means?"

"How should *I* know?" Amy replied. "I've got my own dreams to worry about."

"Well, *excuse me*," Tasha said.

Amy sighed. "Sorry. I didn't mean to snap at you. I guess I'm just not sleeping enough." She glanced at the clock by her bed. "Wow, I'm late! Tasha, why didn't you tell me to get up?" She leaped out of bed and ran toward the bathroom.

"It's not my fault," Tasha yelled after her.

She headed downstairs. Nancy was putting a carton of

juice on the breakfast table in the kitchen. "Morning!" she called out to Tasha. "I'm in a mad rush today; I've got an early meeting at the university. Where's Amy?"

"She's coming," Tasha said. "She overslept."

Eric placed a box of cereal on the table. "At least Amy never has to worry about being late for school. All she has to do is go into fast motion."

Amy might have put herself in high gear upstairs, but for once she wasn't fast enough. The others had finished their breakfast by the time she arrived in the kitchen.

"Amy, have some cereal before you leave," her mother urged.

"I'm not hungry," Amy replied. "And there's no time."

"Amy, you have to eat something," Nancy insisted. "I don't want you going off to school with an empty stomach. Take a granola bar and eat it on the way."

"I said, I'm *not* hungry!"

Nancy was taken aback by Amy's sharp voice. "I'll take it," Tasha said quickly. "C'mon, guys, let's go." Outside, she couldn't keep from saying something to Amy about her tone. "You really shouldn't talk to your mother like that," she said reprovingly.

"She's my mother and I'll talk to her any way I want!"

The force of her voice made Tasha step back. Eric too looked startled.

"You feeling okay?" he asked.

"I'm fine," Amy replied. Then she grinned. "Hey, lighten up, you guys. I've heard you both say worse things to your own mother!"

Tasha tried to smile, and she changed the subject. But after a few moments, a low rumble in the skies made her look up. "Uh-oh. Does anyone have an umbrella?"

"I don't," Amy said. "Why?"

"It's going to rain. Didn't you hear that thunder?"

Amy just stared at her. It gave Tasha the funniest feeling. "Are you feeling okay?"

"Stop asking me that!"

At just that moment, the first few drops began to fall, and they raced the rest of the way to school without speaking. Once inside, they separated to go to their homerooms, and Tasha didn't see Amy again until lunch.

Tasha found her friend sitting at their usual cafeteria table, a dark expression on her face. Tasha was about to ask her if she felt okay, but she caught herself in time. "Hi," she said. "Aren't you going to get lunch?"

Amy shook her head. Tasha dropped her books on the table. "I'll be right back."

Once Tasha had returned with a lunch tray, Amy actually volunteered a reason for her discomfort. "The creepiest thing happened last period in geography. There was a substitute, who called on me and asked me to name the capital of Ecuador. And I didn't know it."

"*I* don't know the capital of Ecuador," Tasha said.

"But I read the chapter just last night," Amy told her. "It should be right there in my head."

Tasha shrugged. "Nobody's perfect."

Amy was silent for a second, and then she said, "*I* am. At least, I'm supposed to be."

"Everyone's entitled to a bad day once in a while," Tasha told her. "You're probably hungry. You didn't eat that granola bar this morning. Why don't you go get a tray? There's tuna salad and you like that."

"Yeah, all right." Amy got up and went to join the cafeteria line. Tasha watched until she disappeared, then began to eat her own lunch. But she put the fork down when Jeanine and her almost-as-awful friend Linda Riviera stopped by the table.

"Tasha," Jeanine said in a voice that dripped with honey, "I want to ask you something. It's about Amy."

Tasha's eyebrows came together suspiciously. "What about Amy?"

Jeanine spoke in a solemn whisper. "We're so worried

about her. She's been acting *very* strange. I mean, stranger than usual. What's wrong with her?"

"There's nothing wrong with Amy," Tasha said sharply.

"Oh, no?" Jeanine asked. "Look at her now."

Tasha turned to see Amy emerging from the line with a tray in her hands. The tray seemed to be shaking. Amy herself appeared to be swaying. Then the tray dropped from her hands.

Linda gasped. Then, as Amy's tuna salad mixed with her spilled milk on the floor, she said, "That's disgusting!"

Tasha jumped up and ran over to her friend. "What happened?" She knelt down to clean up the mess.

"Nothing. It's no big deal," Amy said quickly. She bent down too, picked up the tray, and carried it to the conveyor belt. Tasha watched as she started back toward their table—and bumped smack into another student.

"Hey, look where you're going!" the guy snapped.

"Sorry," Amy said faintly. "I didn't see you." She joined Tasha, and together they went back to the table. Jeanine and Linda were waiting for them.

Jeanine spoke in a loud voice. "Amy, what's the matter with you? That was really clumsy."

"Nothing's the matter," Amy retorted.

"Oh, really!" Jeanine tilted her head and smiled a mean smile. "Amy Candler! Are you on drugs?"

"No, of course not!"

Linda piped up, "Well, something's wrong with you. But we've known that for ages." In a fit of giggles, the two girls walked away.

Tasha looked at her best friend. As she sat down, Amy's face was flushed. "I feel so stupid."

"You're just having a bad day," Tasha repeated lamely.

"I don't *have* bad days," Amy replied. She chewed on her thumbnail. "You heard Jeanine just now. . . ."

"Oh, come on," Tasha remonstrated. "Don't pay any attention to her."

"But what she said about drugs . . . maybe I *am* on drugs."

"Amy! I think you'd know if you were taking drugs!"

"But what if somebody slipped me something without my even knowing it?"

"That's crazy," Tasha said. "You haven't put anything in your mouth all day."

"It's not just today," Amy murmured. "I've been feeling weird for a while." She sucked her breath in sharply. "Ohmigod."

"What?"

"Saturday night at Ace's Space! Somebody could have poisoned that raspberry drink."

Tasha was bewildered. "Someone like who? Who would want to do that to you? Jeanine wasn't even there!"

"But maybe . . . maybe it wasn't just me. Maybe there were drugs in all the drinks!"

Tasha searched her friend's face for a sign that she was joking. She saw nothing amusing there. "Amy . . . that's ridiculous. I drank that raspberry stuff; so did Eric; so did everyone. And we're all feeling one hundred percent."

Amy stared at her with the darkest look Tasha had ever seen on her face. "Are you sure about that?" Amy asked. Then, suddenly, she pushed back her chair, stood up, and started walking away.

"Amy, wait!" Tasha called after her friend's rapidly retreating figure. But Amy kept on walking as if she hadn't even heard her.

five

So this is a headache, Amy thought. She'd never had a headache before in her life, but this pounding sensation couldn't be anything else.

She put a hand to her forehead and rubbed it. Taking her hand away, she noted with surprise that it was wet. She was sweating. Had she ever perspired like this before? She couldn't remember. Ducking into a rest room, she went directly to a sink and splashed cold water on her face.

What was she so upset about anyway? Tasha, of course. Her best friend could be so annoying. But now she couldn't remember how or why Tasha had annoyed her.

She *did* remember that her next class was French and that she would need to collect the textbook from her locker. Since she'd left the cafeteria before the lunch period was over, the halls were quiet as she made her way to the corridor where her locker was.

Her locker was a bottom one, so she knelt to open it. She knew the combination so well that she didn't have to think. Her hand automatically spun the dial to twenty-four, then around twice the other way, stopping at five, and then a short turn to ten. She jerked the locker handle upward.

Nothing happened.

Frowning, she tried it again. Twenty-four, five, ten. But again, she couldn't pull the locker open.

This was crazy. She'd been working this combination at least twice a day since school started. She didn't have to be a clone with super-powers to remember her combination. Hardly anyone ever forgot their locker combination.

Maybe the door was stuck. She started banging on it and shaking the handle. She was so preoccupied that she didn't hear the bell ring or the hordes of students tramping through the corridor. But one of them approached her.

"Hey, what are you doing at my locker?" a boy asked angrily.

"It's *my* locker," she said, looking up. "I'm trying to get it open."

"Oh yeah? What's your locker number?"

"One seventy-three," she replied automatically. That was a number she didn't even have to remember—it was right there in front of her. But as the boy jabbed his finger at the label, it seemed to dissolve. And then the label read 175.

"Oh," she said faintly. "I—I—Never mind." She moved to the next locker, opened it easily, and extracted her French textbook. How could she have been so stupid?

She didn't have time to think about that now. The bell was ringing. She ran down the hall and made it into the room.

Only it wasn't her French class. A totally unfamiliar group of kids stared at her.

"Oh! Sorry." She ran back out and looked around wildly for the French class she'd been going to every weekday for the past three months.

Madame Duquesne was in the middle of giving instructions when Amy burst in. "Amy!" she said in surprise. "*Tu es en retard!* You are late!"

"*Excusez-moi,*" Amy murmured, and took her seat.

Fortunately for her, the class was giving oral reports that week, and she'd already given hers. So she spent the class time trying to figure out why she was feeling—and why she was acting—so strange.

Had she fallen lately and hit her head? Even though she had a superior genetic structure, she wasn't invulnerable to injury. But in her experience, every time she'd been hurt, bruised, cut, scratched, or anything like that, the injury had healed in minutes. And she had no memory of hurting herself lately. Unless . . . Unless she'd been walking in her sleep, had fallen, and had a concussion. That was possible, considering how badly she'd been sleeping . . . all those awful nightmares . . . watching herself disappear in her own dreams . . .

"Amy! Amy!"

Someone was calling her. She blinked twice and realized that it was Madame Duquesne. The teacher was looking at her in concern.

"Oui?"

"Amy . . ." And then Madame Duquesne started to speak very quickly. Amy looked at her blankly.

It was way too much French, too fast and far too sophisticated for Amy to understand, and she told the teacher this in French. "Madame Duquesne, excusez-moi, je ne comprends pas," she said.

"Amy, I was speaking to you in English."

Amy looked at her in disbelief.

Now Madame Duquesne seemed really disturbed. "Amy, are you taking any medication?" she asked.

"No."

But then her super-hearing kicked in. And way behind her, she heard her classmates whispering, "She's on drugs. Amy Candler is a junkie."

"I am *not!*" she yelled.

This time Madame Duquesne spoke in recognizable English. "Amy, I want you to go to the clinic." She wrote something on a piece of paper and beckoned for Amy to come to her desk. Amy rose on unsteady legs, made her way to the front, accepted the note, and left the room.

But she had absolutely no intention of going to the school clinic. Suddenly she believed what was being whispered about her—that she was drugged. Nothing else could explain her confusion. And in the past few days, the only time she'd eaten or drunk anything away from home was at Ace's Space. Something had happened there, she was sure of it.

Then a tiny voice of reason struggled to be heard way back in her mind. A voice that was trying to penetrate the chaos and confusion.

Why would Ace Tolliver want to drug you? He's a rich, well-known businessman. He doesn't know you. He never saw you before Saturday night. You mean nothing to him.

Then she heard the other voice, the voice she'd been hearing all day.

But maybe you do mean something to him. He could be with the organization.

Of course! That made perfect sense. The organization had all kinds of spies. Why not a tycoon? Maybe he'd opened the club for the sole purpose of getting his hands on Amy, Number Seven! She'd always suspected the organization of being a worldwide conspiracy.

Long ago she'd memorized both Eric's and Tasha's class schedules. Thank goodness that memory didn't fail her. She hurried down the hall, up the stairs, and down another hall. Finally she reached Eric's room.

The door was closed, but like all the classroom doors at Parkside, this one had a small glass window. She didn't dare knock. For all she knew, the teacher could be part of the conspiracy too.

She could see Eric through the window. She stared at him, willing him to look her way.

Eventually he did. She watched as he raised his hand and asked to be excused.

The teacher gave him a rest room pass and he came

out into the corridor. "What's the matter?" he asked her, shutting the door behind him.

Amy spoke rapidly. "I know what's wrong with me. I've been drugged. Ace Tolliver poisoned my raspberry drink at the club."

Eric looked at her in disbelief. "Amy!"

"I don't have time to explain now. I have to do something right away."

"Like what?"

"I'm not sure . . . talk to the police? Maybe I should go to the mayor's office. I could call the FBI. Or the CIA. What do you think?"

Eric looked a little frightened. "Amy, this is crazy. Ace Tolliver doesn't want to kill you."

"Oh, I know that," Amy assured him. "He wants to take me alive. He's going to deliver me to the organization, where they can replicate me a thousand times and make an Amy army."

"Amy . . . I think we should call your mother." Eric's face was ashen. "You're not being yourself. I think you're ill."

"Oh, don't be ridiculous," Amy snapped. "Nothing's wrong with me. I'm never sick. Now, do you want to come with me to the police or don't you?"

Eric took her arm. "Let's go to the office and call your mother."

"Oh, Eric," Amy said sadly. "Are you one of them too?"

"One of who?"

Amy didn't bother to explain. She jerked her arm free and took off.

Her legs felt strangely heavy, but she could still run faster than Eric. She heard his footsteps fade as she rounded the corner and tore out of the school. From the corner of her eye, she saw Tasha staring at her through the window of her classroom as she passed.

But Amy didn't stop or wave. Because now she suspected that Tasha was in on the conspiracy too. They all were. That was why the Morgans had left town. That was why Amy's mother had taken the new job. It was all part of the conspiracy to trap Amy. She wasn't sure how the parts of the puzzle fit together, but she knew there had to be a connection. She was on her own. She couldn't trust anyone, not even her own mother.

A while later she was panting heavily and had to stop to catch her breath. Now, where was she? She stared at the street sign until it came into focus. Prince Street. Of course, that was where she intended to go. To Ace's Space, to locate Ace Tolliver and confront him. To find the poison or the drugs or whatever he had put in her raspberry drink so she would have evidence to take to the police and the mayor and the FBI and the CIA. They'd listen to her if she had real, solid evidence.

The building seemed quiet, but she knew better. He was in there; maybe they all were; maybe this was the headquarters for the entire organization that was out to get her. She started toward the front door but thought better of it. They could be lying in wait for her. She had to be more discreet.

Swiftly she moved around to the side of the building. Crouching down, she was able to peer through a basement window.

There was no sign of Ace Tolliver, or anyone else for that matter. The place was deserted.

But of course it would be deserted. An organization attempting to take over the world wouldn't be hanging out in a teen club. And then she remembered something Ace Tolliver had told them Saturday night. He owned the whole place! The organization could be anywhere in this building!

There was a fire escape. The bottom of it hung about ten feet above the ground, but she could jump that high easily. Well, maybe not so easily. It took her five attempts before she was able to grasp the bottom rungs. Then she began to climb. That wasn't easy either. She found her hands unable to grip the bars tightly. She slipped a couple of times, and her body felt unusually heavy as she tried to hoist herself upward.

Still, she persevered, refusing to let her alarming condition affect her progress up the fire escape. It's the drugs, she kept telling herself. That's why I'm weak. Once the drugs are out of my system, I'll be fine. She was feeling dizzy now, and she didn't dare look down, but her determination was still strong. Silently she began to chant: I'm Amy, Number Seven, I'm Amy, Number Seven, no one can hurt me, I'm perfect.

But her eyesight wasn't so perfect anymore. At the fifth-floor window she saw a flicker of movement inside a room, but it was blurry. She squinted and focused her eyes and stared at the image of a man . . . yes, it was Ace Tolliver. He was sitting behind a desk, talking on the telephone.

The window was closed, so she couldn't hear what he was saying, but she knew how to read lips. She concentrated on Tolliver's mouth as he spoke into the phone.

But nothing made sense. Maybe he was speaking a foreign language. She pressed her face closer to the window.

Her movement must have made a noise, because Tolliver looked up. His eyes widened in shock.

Amy's heartbeat accelerated. She had to get away—

but where should she go? Up? Down? Would she be safer on the roof or the ground? Why couldn't she decide? Why was she feeling so confused?

Tolliver had opened the window, and he was yelling at her. But she only knew he was yelling because his mouth was open wide. She could barely hear him. She caught only a few phrases—something like "What are you doing?"

He reached out and grabbed her by the shoulders. She struggled—at least, she thought she was struggling. But either she wasn't struggling very hard, or Ace Tolliver was a lot stronger than he looked. In any case, she felt herself being pulled through the window and inside the room.

"No!" she screamed. "You can't take me! I'm Amy, Number Seven. I'm perfect. I'm stronger than you are!"

But Tolliver didn't believe her, and why should he? She was like a limp rag in his arms. Her arms, her legs . . . even her brain was limp. She heard nothing. She saw nothing.

And then she wasn't even thinking anymore.

s**6**x

Tasha had finished her geometry pop quiz well before the allotted time. She knew it made sense to
check her answers, but instead she found herself staring out the window.

That was when she caught sight of Amy running
out of the school building. Something was wrong.
But whatever it was, it couldn't have been too urgent.
Amy was running at a slow, ordinary speed. If there
had been a real emergency, she'd have been running
triple time. Still, she had been acting awfully weird at
lunch. . . .

Tasha gazed around the room. All the students were

still busily taking their tests. Her eyes moved to the door, and she practically jumped out of her seat. Eric's face was plastered against the little pane of glass.

When he realized she had seen him, his mouth formed silent words. Tasha didn't need to be a lip-reader to know what he wanted. She rose and went to the teacher's desk.

"May I have a rest room pass, please?"

Out in the corridor, she could see that Eric was extremely upset, and he began speaking to her rapidly.

"Something's wrong with Amy—" he began.

"You're telling me," Tasha interrupted, but Eric kept talking.

"No, I mean really. She came by my class just now and was talking like a crazy person. All about how she was drugged by Ace Tolliver, and how he's in some kind of conspiracy with the organization, and how they're all out to get her. She said she was going to the police and the FBI and the CIA. I'm telling you, Tasha, she was scaring me!"

Now Tasha was seriously alarmed. For Eric to declare to his kid sister that he was actually scared, he had to have been totally freaked by Amy's behavior. "Should we call her mother?"

"That's what I tried to do," Eric admitted. "But she's not home and the person I talked to at the university didn't know where she is. I think we should try to find Amy ourselves."

Tasha agreed. Now they had to figure out how to leave school without encountering any trouble. Fortunately, she had long ago devised a plan for just such an emergency, and she put it into motion. She went downstairs to the gym, where a bank of pay phones stood outside in the hallway. She dialed the number of the school.

When the school secretary answered, Tasha deepened her voice to its lowest register. "Hello, this is Mrs. Morgan. Tasha and Eric Morgan will be signing out of school early to go to dental appointments."

Then she ran back upstairs to meet Eric in the principal's office, where they both tried to look like miserable kids who were off to the dentist. Once out of the school building, they walked rapidly and silently until they were half a mile away.

"Where are we going?" Tasha asked.

Eric stopped. "I don't know. To the police station?"

"No way," Tasha declared firmly. "We can't let Amy get that kind of attention, Eric, you know that!"

"That's where she said she might go," Eric told her.

"No, she didn't go to the police," Tasha said. "That's not like Amy."

"But Amy's not being like Amy," Eric pointed out.

He was right. But even so, Tasha had to believe that some spark of normal thinking was still going on in Amy's head. She tried to think the way Amy would think. If Amy thought someone was out to get her, she wouldn't run away or beg for assistance. She'd want to confront the danger on her own.

"Let's find Ace Tolliver," Tasha said.

They had no idea where the tycoon's headquarters might be, so they decided to go Ace's Space. Even if Tolliver wasn't there, someone should be able to tell them where to find him.

It took them forty minutes to get to Prince Street. Along the way, Tasha asked Eric to tell her exactly what Amy had said. The details Eric provided did nothing to ease her concern.

"I'm telling you, Tasha, she's sick," he insisted.

"But Amy doesn't get sick," she protested.

"She doesn't get sick the way *we* get sick," he corrected her. "She doesn't get the flu or colds or measles. But who knows what kind of illness can happen in *her* body?"

Tasha didn't want to know. Months ago, when Amy had first begun to develop her unusual abilities and no one knew why, Tasha had blamed Amy's changes on puberty. Maybe Amy's strange new behavior was something to do with puberty too, some sort of special puberty only a clone went through.

They were approaching the building on Prince Street now, and Eric's pace had perceptibly slowed.

"What's the matter?" Tasha asked.

"I feel kind of weird," Eric admitted. "Exactly what am I going to say to Tolliver? 'Better watch out, because my girlfriend is after you'? He's gonna think I'm nuts."

Tasha spoke sternly. "It seems to me you should be more worried about your girlfriend than what Ace Tolliver thinks. Besides, he probably won't even want to see you."

"Yes he will," Eric declared. "He wants me to be on his advisory panel, remember?"

Personally, Tasha thought Eric was being way too optimistic. She strongly doubted they'd even get taken seriously by the guard at the door of the building.

But she was in for a surprise. The guard actually listened when Eric gave his name and said they wanted to see Mr. Tolliver. And it turned out that Tolliver was in the building.

The guard moved away from them and spoke into a phone. Then he turned back to them. "Fifth floor," he said, pointing to an elevator.

When the elevator doors opened on the fifth floor, Ace Tolliver was waiting for them. He didn't offer them a welcoming smile, but he did appear relieved to see them. "She's in here," he said.

They followed him into a spacious office, where Tasha let out a soft shriek. "Amy!" She ran to the girl on the floor and knelt down beside her. Eric followed her.

"Amy!" he cried hoarsely. But there was no response from the still figure.

"I thought I recognized her," Tolliver said. "She was with you kids at the opening on Saturday night." His brow furrowed. "Bright like a candle," he murmured. "Candler. Amy Candler, right?"

Tasha looked at Tolliver fiercely. "What did you do to her?"

Tolliver seemed taken aback. "I didn't do anything!" he protested. "I found her scratching at my window."

"But you're on the fifth floor!" Tasha exclaimed. "How did she get up here?" Then she gasped. "Ohmigod. Can she fly now?"

"Tasha!" Eric said.

Tolliver was looking at Tasha as if she was some kind of nut. "Your friend must have climbed up the fire escape," he said. "I opened the window and pulled her in. Then she passed out."

"Did she say anything before she fainted?" Eric asked.

"Not a word," Tolliver replied.

Tasha could see the relief on Eric's face, and it made her mad. He was still more concerned about Tolliver's opinion than he was about Amy! And Amy was lying here unconscious! She could be—

But Eric had taken her wrist. "Her pulse feels okay," he said.

"What are you, a doctor?" Tasha snapped.

"I was just about to call an ambulance," Tolliver told them.

"No!" Eric blurted out. "Don't do that!"

"Amy's mother doesn't like doctors," Tasha explained. "Or hospitals."

Tolliver nodded slowly. "I see. Is it some kind of religious belief?"

Tasha was glad to be provided with an excuse. "Yeah, sort of." She bent down and spoke directly into her best friend's ear. "Amy. Amy, can you hear me?" There was still no response.

"Well, we have to do something," Tolliver said. "She can't just lie there. We have to get her home." He picked up his phone and punched in some numbers. "George? Call my driver and tell him to be out front immediately." Then Tolliver took off his suit jacket and flexed his muscles. "Okay, let's go."

He bent down and picked Amy up easily. Tasha couldn't help being impressed with the care he took in carrying her, making sure she didn't hit the door frame as he maneuvered her out into the hall.

A long black limousine waited outside the building. Gently Tolliver laid Amy's unconscious body on a seat. Tasha and Eric sat facing her. Then Tolliver got into the front seat next to the driver. "Where does she live?" he asked, turning around.

Eric provided the address, and the driver took off. "Has your friend ever fainted like this before?" Tolliver asked them.

"No, never," Tasha answered firmly. She tried not to think about the time in New York when Amy had passed out at the dinner honoring contestants in the National Essay Competition. But that was different, of course. Amy had been poisoned.

Of course, drugs were a kind of poison, and Tasha knew that Amy was convinced she'd been poisoned. But as Tasha examined the tycoon's expression of concern and thought about his actions just now in the office, she had to admit that her brother was right. Amy was thinking like a crazy person. Tolliver's club was clean.

"What was she doing on my fire escape?" Tolliver asked.

"No idea," Eric said.

"Haven't a clue," Tasha echoed.

"Is she . . . normal?" Tolliver asked.

"Absolutely," Eric replied.

"Totally," Tasha declared.

"But you said she thinks she can fly," Tolliver remarked to Tasha.

"That's just my sister talking nonsense," Eric said quickly. "She's the one who's not too normal."

For once Tasha didn't argue.

The limousine entered their condominium complex, and Eric directed the driver to Amy's front door. Nancy Candler had just pulled into the driveway. Getting out of her car, she looked at the limousine curiously. When Tolliver gathered Amy from the backseat and lifted her out, Nancy turned white.

"What happened?"

Tasha and Eric tried to explain as Tolliver carried Amy inside the house and up to her bedroom, where he laid her gently on the bed. Fortunately, Nancy was too concerned about Amy's condition to ask many questions about what her daughter had been doing in Tolliver's office. She just thanked Tolliver for his kindness.

As soon as he was out of the house, Nancy went to the phone and dialed. "David? Something's wrong with Amy! Could you come over right away?"

"Was that Dr. Hopkins?" Tasha asked her.

Nancy nodded. "I don't know what I'd do if he wasn't here in the area," she said. "I can't call a regular doctor." She sat down on the bed next to Amy and felt her forehead. "She's burning up. I just can't believe it. She's never had a fever in her life."

Tasha had seen Ms. Candler upset and worried many times before. But she'd never seen Amy's mother look this frightened. It made Tasha feel frightened too.

She and Eric busied themselves making cold compresses from washcloths to lay on Amy's forehead. Dr. Hopkins must have broken every speed limit to get to the house, because it wasn't very long before he was ringing the doorbell.

Eric let him in. Then he and Tasha were ordered out of the bedroom while Dr. Hopkins examined Amy, with her mother watching. Tasha followed Eric to the kitchen, where they both slumped down at the table.

"Eric," Tasha murmured. "I'm scared."

"Yeah," Eric replied. "Me too."

They said no more, but those simple words created a bond Tasha hadn't felt with her brother in a long time. They sat in silence and waited.

When Dr. Hopkins and Nancy finally came downstairs and into the kitchen, Tasha and Eric both looked up anxiously. The expressions on the adults' faces didn't lift their spirits. Dr. Hopkins told them what he had found.

"Amy has a very high fever," he said. "It's the kind that could kill an ordinary person."

Tasha moaned. Nancy came over and hugged her.

"But Amy isn't an ordinary person," Amy's mother said fiercely. "We have to keep telling ourselves that. What could be serious for any one of us may not be serious for her." She filled a bowl with ice cubes and water and went back upstairs.

"How are you going to treat her?" Eric asked the doctor.

"We're going to get her fever down," Dr. Hopkins answered. "I've taken some blood, skin, and hair samples for testing back at my office. That will let me know if there's been any alteration in her genetic structure. Is there anything you two can tell me about the way she's been feeling lately?"

"She hasn't been herself," Eric admitted. "She's been getting tired, and she's not as strong or quick as she usually is."

"She said she thinks she was drugged," Tasha said.

The doctor seemed interested in that information. "How? What kind of drugs?"

"I don't know. She said there was something in the soda she had at the teen club we all went to Saturday night."

"Which is ridiculous," Eric said quickly. "We all drank the same soda, and the rest of us feel fine."

"But we're different than Amy," Tasha argued. "Maybe she reacted to the drugs differently."

"There were no drugs!" Eric declared. "Ace Tolliver wouldn't allow any drugs in his teen club!"

"But Amy thought she was drugged!" Tasha shot back.

"That's because she's sick and she's not thinking rationally!"

"Yeah, well, maybe the drugs are what did that to her!"

"She wasn't drugged!" Eric practically shrieked.

"Okay, okay," Dr. Hopkins interrupted. "I know you're both upset, but you have to stay calm. We have no idea what's going on here. Amy could be going through some process that's totally normal for her special physical condition. We'll just have to wait and see. I'll run as many tests as I can."

Eric spoke hesitantly. "Dr. Hopkins, could you—could you maybe call in a specialist for another opinion?"

Dr. Hopkins wasn't offended at the suggestion. He smiled sadly. "There are no specialists for a person like Amy."

He went upstairs to consult once again with Nancy, and then he left, promising to call in with test results later. Nancy remained by Amy's bedside, coming down only to ask Tasha and Eric if they were hungry.

They weren't. No one wanted any dinner that evening.

Three hours later the call from Dr. Hopkins came in. Nancy spoke with him on the kitchen phone. All Tasha and Eric could hear was her murmurs of "Uh-huh" and "All right" and "If you think so." Then she hung up.

Tasha and Eric looked at her expectantly.

"The tests didn't reveal anything," she told them. "But at least they ruled out some possibilities. There's no viral or bacterial infection. There's no sign of any cellular damage or disorder."

"What about drugs?" Tasha asked.

"He tested the blood for every possible chemical compound," Nancy said. "There are no drugs in her system, and there's no evidence that any drugs have ever been administered to her."

Tasha looked at her brother. She expected him to gloat. But she could tell that he didn't feel triumphant. For once he didn't say "I told you so."

He was still just as scared as she was.

seven

Cold. Very, very cold. And dark, like pitch-black night. All she saw was the moon, but not a full moon, just a little sliver. A crescent moon.

Was she dead? Maybe . . . a man was approaching her. He seemed alive, but she knew better. It was Mr. Devon, a man of mystery who used to turn up in her life every now and then to point her in a new direction. Now he was dead, which meant she must be dead too. Did he have something to tell her?

You shouldn't have done it, Amy. You shouldn't have done it.

I shouldn't have done what?

But Mr. Devon was gone. Another dead man had taken his place.

Dr. J! Do you have something to tell me?

I'm sorry, Amy. I'm very sorry.

Sorry for what?

But he was gone too.

At least she wasn't cold anymore. In fact, she was warm. She was enclosed in glass, and she was getting warmer. Too warm . . .

eight

Eric slumped in his seat and drummed his fingers restlessly on the desk. In the front of the classroom, a teacher was talking about a crucial turning point in the Civil War. The teacher was solemn and dramatic as he described the dead bodies on a battlefield, the thousands of casualties, but it meant nothing to Eric. The only body he could see was Amy's, lying on a bed, so still, so pale. Fragile. That was a word Eric had never thought he'd use to describe Amy, but that was how she had looked that morning. Like she could break into pieces.

A coma. Amy was in a coma.

Dr. Hopkins didn't know how she'd gotten that way, or how he could bring her out of it. Eric had pleaded with him to do something. But Dr. Hopkins was helpless. All they could do was wait. And waiting was something Eric had never been very good at.

From across the room, his pal Kyle was eyeing him curiously. Eric sat up straighter and tried to look like he was paying attention. He didn't want Kyle, or anyone, to ask him any questions that day. He could still hear Ms. Candler's warning to him and Tasha as they left for school that morning.

"Don't talk about this. If anyone asks where Amy is, say she has a mild case of bronchitis. Nothing serious. But she's not feeling well and she doesn't want any visitors."

Kyle was waiting for him at the classroom door after the bell rang. "What's up, man? You're looking bummed out."

"I'm okay," Eric said.

"You don't look okay. Wanna come to the Space with me after school?"

"The Space?" Eric asked blankly.

"Yeah, Ace's Space. I stopped by yesterday with a couple of guys, and the joint was jumping. You look like you could use some fun."

Fun was the last thing on Eric's mind. "I gotta go

make a phone call," he muttered, and took off in the opposite direction. He went downstairs toward the gym, to the bank of pay telephones.

Nancy Candler answered on the first ring. "Hello?" Even in that one word, Eric could hear the tension in her voice.

"It's me—Eric. How's Amy?"

"There's no change, Eric."

"No change at all?"

"No change at all."

"But she's not any worse, right?"

"She's no worse, and she's no better. She's exactly the same."

"What does Dr. Hopkins say?" he asked.

Nancy's tone was getting irritable. "Eric, he said there's no change."

"Maybe I should come home."

"There's nothing for you to do here, and you need to stay at school. Is that the bell I'm hearing in the background?"

It was, and now he'd be late for Spanish. Which meant he would get a demerit, which meant he'd have to stay after school for detention, which meant he'd be getting back to Amy even later. Feeling even more frustrated, he said goodbye quickly and ran to his class.

At least he had one tiny stroke of good luck. There

was a substitute in Spanish, and she didn't appear to be familiar with the detention system. She was taking roll when he walked in and barely glanced up. And she had no lesson plan, so they were assigned to read silently from their textbooks for the next forty minutes.

The Spanish words on Eric's page could have been Greek as far as he was concerned. But at least his depression was turning into a more active emotion—anger. What was Dr. Hopkins doing for Amy anyway? Just watching and waiting?

Eric didn't have much experience with medicine, but he'd seen enough TV shows to know that seriously ill patients were always hooked up to bags that pumped medicine into their veins. Why wasn't Amy getting medications? Why wasn't Dr. Hopkins doing more tests on her, taking X rays, *something*? Probably because he didn't know what he was doing. He might have been some hotshot doctor twelve years ago, but all he'd been doing lately was stitching up cuts and giving allergy shots. He was a small-town doctor who sent any really sick patients to specialists.

With all the advances in medical science, there had to be someone out there who would know what to do for Amy, someone who would take action, who wouldn't just sit around twiddling his thumbs and watching her sink deeper and deeper into her coma.

Eric had to talk to someone. But there was only one person he could safely discuss Amy with.

There was an unwritten social rule at lunchtime in the Parkside Middle School cafeteria—boys sat with boys, girls sat with girls, and the grades didn't mix. For once, Eric was going to have to break this rule.

Tasha was sitting with a couple of classmates, who looked startled when Eric approached. "Family stuff," he muttered as an excuse, and motioned to Tasha to follow him to a corner behind the garbage cans, where they could have a little privacy.

"I called Amy's mother a little while ago," he told her. "She said Amy's the same."

"I know," Tasha replied. "I called too, and I talked to Dr. Hopkins."

"What did he say?"

"Nothing much. Just that there's been no change."

Eric ran his fingers through his hair. "What do you think of Dr. Hopkins?"

"He's nice," Tasha said.

"Nice." Eric snorted. "Nice doesn't mean he's a great doctor. You know what kind of a doctor he is? He gives tetanus shots and pierces ears. Amy deserves better. I think Ms. Candler should find a specialist."

Tasha looked troubled. "But Eric, she can't bring in another doctor. It isn't safe. Imagine what could happen if word about Amy got out!"

"But imagine what could happen if she didn't get any treatment," Eric argued. "She could die!"

Tasha gazed at him helplessly. "Eric, I'm just as worried as you are, but what can we do?"

Eric considered that. "I'm going to call Ms. Candler again," he said abruptly.

"We shouldn't keep bothering her," Tasha protested, but Eric was already halfway across the cafeteria and heading to the exit.

Amy's mother sounded even more tired when she answered the phone, and she didn't have any news. "There's no change, Eric. But Dr. Hopkins is still here, and he's watching her."

Watching. A whole lot of good that was going to do. "Ms. Candler, do you think maybe you could call another doctor? You know, like, for a second opinion."

Nancy sighed. "Eric, I know you're worried, but surely you realize that Dr. Hopkins is the only doctor I can trust with Amy. A second opinion is out of the question."

"But maybe Dr. Hopkins isn't the best—"

Amy's mother broke in sharply. "Dr. Hopkins is a very fine doctor, Eric."

Eric hung up. He wasn't surprised that Amy's mother had said that. She had to try to convince herself that she was doing the best for her daughter. Maybe she was right.

But maybe she wasn't. And Eric knew he'd never be able to live with himself if he hadn't done everything in his power to save his girlfriend.

He made a fist with his right hand and slammed it into the palm of his left hand. He felt so helpless. If only he had someone he could talk to, someone he could trust . . . not Tasha. He needed someone older and wiser. . . .

He drew in his breath sharply. Of *course*. Why hadn't he thought of that sooner?

Luckily, Kyle was in his last class of the day. And he was very pleased when Eric announced that he'd be going with him to the Space after all.

nine

Hot, so hot, so very, very hot. Fire all around her. The glass wouldn't protect her much longer. She knew what would happen next. The woman in the white coat would appear, she would open the glass, she would gather Amy in her arms and carry her out of the laboratory. And Amy would call her Mother.

Heat . . . heat and horror.

A crescent moon, consumed by flames . . .

Jeanine Bryant, pointing and laughing . . .

Amys, a row of Amys, marching arm in arm to battle . . .

Mr. Devon's body slumped over the wheel of his car.

Dr. Jaleski's body facedown on his living room floor.

The Wilderness Adventure counselor's body drowned in the river rapids.

The body of Amy, Number Four, lying on a stretcher in a New York hospital.

And now the body of Amy, Number Seven, would join them. Because no one was coming to rescue her.

ten **10**

Tasha had been shocked when Eric told her he was going to the Space. He could read her thoughts in her eyes—how could he even think about going out while his girlfriend lay in a coma? But he couldn't tell her why he was really going, not with Kyle standing right there by his side. Well, let her think he was a self-ish jerk. She'd find out soon enough that he was doing the right thing.

As Kyle had guaranteed, the Space was rocking. Eric could hear the music and the noise coming from the basement when he entered the lobby of the building on Prince Street. The heavyset bouncer waved them toward the basement entrance, and Kyle started in that direction, but Eric hung back.

"I'll meet you down there," he called to Kyle, and went over to the elevator.

Before he could even press the Up button, the bouncer materialized by his side.

"Where do you think you're going?"

"I have to see Mr. Tolliver," Eric said. "It's important."

"Yeah, right. Look, pal, it's downstairs or out of here. That's the choice."

"No, really, he'll see me," Eric insisted. "He knows me. Just call him and tell him Eric Morgan needs to talk to him!" But the bouncer was already hustling him toward the door that led outside.

Then a mobile phone attached to the bouncer's belt began to beep. With one hand still gripping Eric, the bouncer used his other hand to answer it.

"Yes, sir?" A second later he said "Yes, sir" again. Then, to Eric's surprise, the bouncer released his grip. "Tolliver will see you."

"How did he know I was here?"

The guard nodded toward a corner of the ceiling. For the first time, Eric noticed a security camera.

When he got off the elevator on the fifth floor, Ace

Tolliver was waiting for him. "Good to see you, Eric," he said cordially. "How's your friend Amy?"

"Not too good," Eric told him. "That's why I'm here."

Tolliver's brow furrowed, and Eric hastened to explain. "I was wondering if maybe you could give me some advice."

Tolliver stared at him intently. Then he said, "Come into my office."

Once he was seated, Eric realized he had no idea how to tell Tolliver what he needed without exposing Amy's secrets.

"What's wrong with Amy?" Tolliver asked him.

"She's in a coma."

Tolliver's eyebrows shot up. "Is she in a hospital?"

"No . . ."

"Oh, that's right," Tolliver said. "Her mother belongs to a religion that doesn't believe in hospitals or doctors."

"Yes," Eric said, grateful for an excuse to make his request. "The thing is, I really want a doctor to see her. A specialist."

"What kind of specialist?"

Eric hesitated.

Tolliver prodded him. "Amy is . . . unusual, isn't she? She's not like other girls. She's special, right?"

"Why do you say that?"

Tolliver smiled. "Well, obviously she means a great deal to you. So she must be a pretty unique girl."

Eric relaxed. "Right, she's special to me. Not special in any other way, though. Completely normal. I just want to get a really top doctor to look at her."

Tolliver nodded. "I can understand that. But I really shouldn't be meddling in a situation that doesn't concern me. Still, everyone deserves proper medical care, especially if a life is at stake."

"So you'll help?" Eric asked, feeling hopeful.

Tolliver nodded. "I just happen to know Dr. Arnold Vickers. He's a very good friend of mine."

He said this as if the doctor's name was supposed to mean something. So Eric tried to look impressed.

"Arnold is the world's most famous medical authority on comas," Tolliver explained.

Eric brightened. "Oh! Wow, do you think he could take a look at Amy? The only problem is her mother can't know about it. Because of her religion," he added hastily.

"I understand," Tolliver said. "How about this? You let me know when Amy's mother is out of the house. I'll get in touch with Arnold and he'll come right over to look at Amy."

This guy was too fantastic, and Eric was overcome

with gratitude. "Wow, that would be so great. Thank you."

"I'll give you my private mobile phone number," Tolliver said. "Call me anytime."

Eric couldn't exactly say his heart was light when he left Tolliver's office. Still, he felt a whole lot better knowing that there was a doctor out there who just might be able to help Amy.

But he had another problem to contend with. Since Amy had fallen ill, Nancy Candler hadn't left her daughter's side. A world-famous specialist couldn't do much for a patient if he couldn't get near her.

eleven

She was burning.

Amy was consumed by fire. Every genetically engineered cell in her body was in flames. The glass had melted away. She was exposed, vulnerable, totally unprotected.

And then she wasn't even there.

twelve

The local newspaper was on the kitchen table when Tasha arrived home from school. She could hear Nancy Candler moving around upstairs in Amy's room, so she sat down to eat an apple and glance at the paper.

The Parkside Journal didn't try to compete with the big papers in their coverage of major national and world events. So a big chunk of the front page was devoted to an enthusiastic report on Ace's Space.

It's clear that this club is filling a need in the community. Kids from neighboring middle schools are pouring into the Space daily, and the club is packed from immediately after school till closing. Ace Tolliver promises that new clubs opening soon in nearby suburbs will ease the overcrowding.

Parents are enthusiastic about the clubs, which provide a clean, safe, and healthy place for kids to hang out. And the kids are enthusiastic because everything about this club is geared toward their tastes and their idea of fun. The only adults in evidence are the big bodyguards who check kids at the door and keep an eye out for any trouble-makers. This doesn't bother anyone. As one boy put it, "All the big discos have bouncers."

The great Ace Tolliver himself makes frequent tours of the club, though he tries not to draw too much attention to himself. "I don't want to cramp anyone's style," he says with a laugh. "After all, I'm just another grown-up to these kids, no more fun than their own parents!" But of course, if it wasn't for Ace Tolliver, these kids wouldn't be having this much fun at all!

Tasha wrinkled her nose. The reporter was making Ace Tolliver sound like a saint. And she was so annoyed with her brother at that moment, she didn't want to hear or read anything complimentary about Ace's Space. How could Eric go there in a time of crisis? How could he even *think* about having fun?

A crash above her sent Tasha flying out of the kitchen and up the stairs. In the doorway of Amy's bedroom, she froze at the sight that confronted her.

Amy was rolling around on the floor, her arms flailing in the air. Nancy was trying to restrain her. Tasha darted forward and bent down by her friend's heaving body.

"She's having some kind of seizure," Nancy told her in a rush. "She threw herself off the bed. I'm afraid she's going to get hurt!"

Together they tried to hold Amy down. Tasha was almost grateful that the fever had weakened her—in good form, Amy could probably take on both Nancy and Tasha with one hand tied behind her back. But even a feeble Amy was stronger than Tasha. Unprepared, Tasha was knocked backward by the force of Amy's swinging arm and hit her head against the wall.

"Tasha, are you all right?" Nancy cried out.

Tasha staggered back to rejoin them. "I'm okay," she said, trying to avoid being kicked in the face by Amy's feet.

"Eric!" Nancy called out. "Eric, we need your help!"

"Eric's not here," Tasha said. Thank goodness Nancy was too preoccupied to ask where he was. Tasha was so ashamed of him. She and Nancy struggled fiercely to pull Amy back up onto her bed.

Amy's movements became less violent. She started twitching and mumbling. "No good, no good," she muttered. "Tolliver, no good. Go away." Then she sat up suddenly, her eyes wide open. "Go away! Make him go away! Evil! Evil! Evil!"

"She's hallucinating," Nancy said. She was at the phone now, dialing.

Tasha tried to ease Amy back down on the bed. She heard Nancy telling Dr. Hopkins about the situation.

"He'll be here as soon as he can," Nancy said to Tasha, rejoining her at Amy's bedside. Amy was silent now, and her eyes had closed.

Tasha didn't know what was worse—seeing Amy lying as still as a corpse or watching her thrashing around like a crazy person. Amy remained in the former state as they sat by her side and waited for the doctor.

Dr. Hopkins made them both go downstairs while he examined Amy. Nancy went into her little office by the kitchen and shut the door, but Tasha could hear her crying. Tasha huddled alone on the sofa in the living room, cursed her rotten, selfish brother, and tried not to think about a life without Amy.

But when the doctor came back downstairs, he actually appeared to be slightly optimistic. Nancy came out of her office, and they both listened to his report. "I don't know what that was all about," he said. "The seizure and the hallucination. But it could be an indication that she's coming out of her coma."

Tasha thought that sounded good, but Nancy didn't seem terribly relieved. "It's all my fault," she murmured. "If I hadn't taken this new job, I wouldn't have been working so much. I would have been spending more time with Amy. I would have noticed her symptoms earlier."

Dr. Hopkins shook his head. "Don't be so hard on yourself, Nancy. It wouldn't have made any difference. Look, if you really want to do something to help Amy, then get to work now."

"What?" Nancy exclaimed.

"Let's go to the lab at the university and run some more tests. Let's examine some new databases on the Internet and see if there's any new research."

"But I can't leave Amy here alone!" Nancy objected.

"She won't be alone," Tasha offered. "I'm here."

"And I've got a mobile phone," Dr. Hopkins added.

"So if there's any problem, Tasha can get in touch with us right away. Sitting around worrying about Amy isn't going to do her any good. Let's see if we can find out what caused this. Then maybe we can figure out how to cure it."

Nancy was clearly torn. Only when Eric walked through the door did she agree to the doctor's suggestion. "Well, now that the two of you are here," she murmured to Tasha and Eric. Quickly she brought Eric up to date. "Could you kids fix your own dinner? I'll be back in a few hours."

Tasha had been glaring at her brother ever since he'd come in, but she held her tongue until Nancy and Dr. Hopkins left. Then she let him have it. "I can't believe you went to that stupid club when Amy was lying up there, having seizures and hallucinations and . . ." She stopped when she realized that Eric wasn't even listening to her. He was moving toward the kitchen. Tasha followed him.

"This is so typical of you, Eric," she railed on. "Now you're more interested in getting something to eat than going upstairs to see your girlfriend!"

But for once Eric didn't go directly to the refrigerator. Instead, he went to the phone.

"Who are you calling?" Tasha demanded, but Eric

didn't answer her. The look of grim determination on his face was a little scary.

"Mr. Tolliver? This is Eric Morgan. Amy's mother's gone out for a few hours. Do you think that doctor could come over and examine her now?"

Tasha gasped. "Eric!" she shrieked. "What are you doing?"

"Thank you," Eric said into the phone, and hung up. Finally he spoke to Tasha.

"That's why I went to the Space, so I could ask Ace Tolliver for some help. He knows this world-famous specialist, and he's sending him over here to look at Amy."

Tasha was horrified. "A world-famous specialist in *what*? Genetically designed clones? Eric, you didn't tell Tolliver about Amy, did you?"

"No, of course not," Eric said testily. "But I *would* have, if I'd thought it would help. Mr. Tolliver said this Dr. Vickers knows all about comas." He started up the stairs, and Tasha ran after him.

"Are you crazy, Eric? You know we can't let any regular doctor look at Amy! He'll discover what she is. Her secret won't be safe!"

"I don't care," Eric said flatly. "It's better than letting her die."

"But Amy doesn't even trust this Tolliver guy," Tasha went on as they both entered her bedroom. "Just now, when she was having the seizure, she kept screaming that he's evil!"

"Which just shows how ill she is," Eric declared. "She's not being rational; she's not herself." He sat by Amy's side and gazed down at her. She was back in her silent, nearly lifeless state.

"Ms. Candler is going to kill you," Tasha hissed. "Eric, she's the mother of our best friend; she's letting us live here. How can you betray her like this?"

"I'm doing what's best for Amy," Eric replied firmly. He got up and left the room.

Tasha's thoughts were running wild. Should she lock the bedroom door so Eric and the world-famous specialist couldn't get in? No, in Eric's current state, he'd have no problem with breaking down the door. Should she call Amy's mother and Dr. Hopkins? That didn't seem like the right solution either. Nancy was near panic, and Tasha couldn't bear to see her suffer more.

No. She, Tasha Morgan, best friend, would have to save Amy from this invasion of privacy, this possible exploitation. And with a sinking stomach, Tasha realized that there was only one way she could accomplish this task.

Dr. Vickers had never seen Amy before. All he knew

was that he'd be examining a twelve-year-old girl who was in a coma. As for Eric . . . Tasha smiled grimly. If there was one thing she knew for sure about her brother, it was that anything that involved doctors made him nervous. He hadn't even liked hearing the details of their ear-piercing experience. Not to mention the fact that he would be too embarrassed to be in the room while the doctor conducted any kind of intimate examination. He'd probably just direct the doctor to the room and stay downstairs.

She didn't have much time. And now Amy was mumbling again. What if she went into another seizure? How could Tasha possibly do what needed to be done?

She sat next to Amy. "Amy, can you hear me? Amy?"

"Tasha . . . ," Amy murmured.

Encouraged, Tasha kept on talking. "There's danger. I have to hide you."

"Danger . . . ," Amy repeated.

"Yes, danger. Can you move?"

"Danger," Amy said again. "Tolliver. Danger. Evil."

"Yeah, yeah, whatever you say," Tasha said hurriedly. "Tolliver is dangerous and evil. Anyway, he's sending over a doctor to look at you. Amy, I have to get you out of this bed. Don't fight me, okay?"

"Go to police . . ."

"Police? I can't call the police! They won't do anything.

Eric's just being stupid; it's not like something illegal is happening!"

"Police," Amy said again. "Tell police . . . Tolliver . . . drugs . . ."

Tasha sighed. Amy was obviously fixating on the tycoon and the irrational belief that he'd drugged her. But Tasha didn't have time to argue with her hallucinating friend.

It hadn't been easy moving Amy even with Nancy's help. Tasha didn't know how she would do it by herself. But she'd read somewhere that in times of emergency, people found they had strength beyond what was normal.

"Be strong, be strong," she chanted as she pulled Amy by one arm and one leg. At least Amy didn't fight her—she appeared to be completely unconscious again. But it was like pulling a huge dead weight. And though Tasha knew Amy weighed only a hundred pounds, it seemed like she weighed a ton.

Tasha kept on tugging, sliding Amy off the bed and angling herself flat on the floor so Amy's head would land on her stomach.

"Ooof," she grunted as Amy's head fell on her. Then, inch by inch, she dragged Amy across the floor toward the closet. She was almost there when Amy began hallucinating. "Danger," she murmured. "Danger."

"Yes, you're in danger," Tasha muttered grimly. "And I'm trying to save you." Holding Amy with one hand, she used the other to open the closet door.

And then what she had feared happened. Amy started moving, flailing her arms in the air. She was struggling to free herself.

"Amy, don't!" Tasha cried in a panic. "You have to be quiet!"

"Tolliver, danger, police!" Amy gasped.

"Amy, shhh," Tasha pleaded.

Then Amy's eyes shot open wide. "Promise me!"

"Promise you what?" Tasha asked in despair. Because at that minute, she could hear the doorbell ringing downstairs.

"Tell police! Tolliver! Promise me. Promise me!"

"I promise, I promise," Tasha cried out. "Now be quiet!"

To her amazement, Amy did as she was told. She became silent and went absolutely limp, and Tasha was able to shove her into the walk-in closet.

She could hear Eric downstairs, directing the doctor to the bedroom. With no time to spare, she whipped off her own clothes and pulled on her nightgown. As the footsteps got closer, she dived into Amy's bed.

Waves of fear passed over her. There was no telling what this specialist was about to do to her. She wasn't scared for her life. It was the thought of needles that terrified her.

Her throat became blocked and she couldn't swallow.

She had to find strength. She had to do this for Amy.

She saw the door handle move and quickly closed her eyes. It took her every ounce of willpower to keep all her features calm and placid.

A shudder went through her as the doctor came in and lifted the bedsheet. She felt the chill of the stethoscope on her chest, and she tried not to wince when he tightened the blood pressure band around her upper arm. He ran something along the soles of her feet that made her toes curl. Then she heard him tearing something open, and she knew with a dread certainty that a needle was being prepared. The cold swab of alcohol against her skin confirmed this.

She concentrated hard again. Think of Amy, think of Amy, you're saving Amy, you're saving Amy . . . She chanted the words mentally like a prayer, hoping they would distract her. They didn't—but somehow she found the power to keep herself still as the needle pierced her skin. Inside, she could hear a silent scream echoing throughout her mind and body, and she was overcome by nausea—but she didn't give any indication of this to the doctor. And when it was all over, she could feel the throbbing from the prick of the needle, but she felt an enormous pride in what she had been able to do for her best friend.

She heard the door open and close, but she waited for the sound of footsteps going down the stairs. As soon as she was satisfied that the doctor wouldn't be coming back, she jumped out of bed and ran to the closet.

Amy lay there in the same position Tasha had left her in, crumpled among the shoes and boxes at the bottom of the closet. Tasha gripped her under the arms and began to pull. Amy stirred.

"Promise me, promise, Tolliver . . . police . . ."

"Yes, yes, I promise," Tasha grunted as she dragged her friend across the room. At least Amy wasn't struggling. But by the time they reached the bed, she was completely unconscious again, which only made it more difficult to hoist her onto the mattress.

Tasha made it just in time. The door opened, and Eric stood there.

"Is she okay?" he asked Tasha.

"No thanks to you," Tasha snapped.

"The doctor said he couldn't make a diagnosis until he's run some tests on her blood," Eric went on.

Tasha didn't reply. So the doctor had taken something out of her instead of putting something in. She wasn't sure if that made her feel better or worse.

"Why are you in your nightgown?" Eric asked. "It's only seven o'clock!"

"I'm tired," Tasha replied coldly. "I want to go to bed early. Would you mind leaving the room now?"

Eric went out, shutting the door behind him. Tasha then went to Amy's desk and pulled out a blank piece of paper and an envelope. She had a promise to keep.

She printed the words clearly.

To whom it may concern:
    This is an anonymous tip. There is a rumor that drugs are being distributed by Ace Tolliver in his teen club, Ace's Space.

She folded the paper, put it in the envelope, and addressed it to the Los Angeles Police Department. She didn't know the street address, but she figured this was enough information to get it where it should go. Not that it mattered. The police probably received hundreds of silly tips like this daily, and it would just end up in a wastebasket.

"Tasha . . ."

"Mmm?" She had found a book of stamps in the drawer and was peeling one off.

"Tasha . . . what's going on?"

She whirled around. Amy was pulling herself up to a

sitting position. She was pale, and she looked very confused, but her eyes were open and alert.

Tasha rushed over to her. "Amy! How do you feel?"

Amy considered the question. "Am I sick?"

"You were," Tasha cried out joyfully. "But you're better now!" She ran to the door and opened it.

"Eric! Eric! Amy's awake!"

thirteen

"**O**h, pooh," Amy moaned in frustration. She ripped a page out of her notebook and crumpled it. Tasha watched with sympathy.

"Math?"

"I don't get it," Amy muttered. "These problems aren't so hard. I don't know why I'm having so much trouble with this stupid homework." She tossed the crumpled paper toward the wastebasket. It didn't go in. Amy grimaced.

"Hey, don't get so upset," Tasha said. "You just came out of a coma two days ago. You're still weak. Give yourself some time to recover."

"I know," Amy sighed. "I shouldn't be so impatient. But I'm not sick anymore and I want to feel normal. Well, my kind of normal."

Tasha pushed her own homework aside. "Are you hungry?" she asked. "I'm starving. What time is it?"

Amy turned to glance at the clock on the nightstand. Then she frowned. "I can't even see my clock from here! Ooh, I hate this! I don't feel like myself!"

"Well, at least you're talking like yourself now," Tasha reminded her comfortingly. "That's a major improvement from two days ago."

Amy grinned. "Was I a real lunatic?"

"Pretty close," Tasha replied. "Do you remember anything?"

"Not much," Amy admitted. "To tell the truth, I can barely remember anything that's happened since the day we got our ears pierced."

Tasha supposed that was a good thing. If Amy couldn't remember Tasha's dragging her into the closet, she didn't have to know that Eric had betrayed her. On the other hand, it was too bad that Tasha couldn't tell Amy what a good and true friend she herself had been. But there was another way Tasha could safely point this out.

"I kept that promise," she said mischievously.

"What promise?" Amy wanted to know.

"You kept going on and on about Ace Tolliver being a drug pusher. You made me promise I'd alert the police."

"Oh, no," Amy groaned. "Are you serious? I said that? And you told the police?"

"I made you a promise and I kept it," Tasha said virtuously. "Anyway, it's no big deal. The police aren't going to pay any attention to an anonymous letter that contains no evidence."

"I sincerely hope not," Amy said. She started on another math problem and made no effort to muffle her groans.

"Well," Tasha said, trying not to sound smug, "now you know how the rest of us ordinary folks have to suffer over homework."

"I'll definitely have more sympathy for you from now on," Amy assured her. She sighed deeply. "I wish Dr. Hopkins would get here. Maybe he'll be able to tell me how much longer I have to go on like this."

Tasha couldn't help reminding her of something. "You used to say you wished you could be normal."

"I've changed my mind," Amy said darkly. "No offense, but I've been normal long enough, thank you very much. I want my powers back."

"There's the doorbell—maybe that's Dr. Hopkins now," Tasha said. "I'll get it." She ran downstairs and opened the door to the smiling doctor.

"How's our patient today?" he asked Tasha as he came in.

"Fine," Tasha said. "Well, the same as she was yesterday. She's starting to get a little antsy. When will her powers start coming back?"

The doctor didn't answer. "Hi, Nancy," he said to Amy's mom, who had come out of the kitchen.

Tasha didn't miss the long, searching look Amy's mother gave the doctor. He shook his head slightly, and she seemed disturbed. Without saying anything, they went upstairs together.

Tasha was still wondering what was going on when Eric came home. He started immediately for the stairs, but Tasha stopped him. "The doctor's there," she told him. "Speaking of doctors, did you ever get a report from your buddy Ace Tolliver? Did that specialist figure out what was wrong with Amy?"

Eric had the grace to look slightly embarrassed. "Actually, Mr. Tolliver told me that Dr. Vickers said Amy is perfectly healthy. I guess it was pretty stupid, what I did."

"Very stupid," Tasha corrected him, but she couldn't

help smiling. It was nice to know that she herself was perfectly healthy.

"Well, it doesn't matter now," Eric said. "She's all better, right? I mean, just about."

Tasha would have agreed, but she was still thinking about the strange look Ms. Candler and Dr. Hopkins had exchanged before going upstairs. Did they know something she didn't know?

Apparently so. Because when they came downstairs, they both looked extremely sober. And when Eric started up the stairs, Ms. Candler said, "Not right now, Eric." Then she asked Tasha and Eric to sit down with her and the doctor at the kitchen table.

"As Amy's closest friends, there's something you need to know," she said. "Dr. Hopkins has done some tests on Amy, and . . . well, I'll let him tell you what he learned."

"I've examined Amy's cellular structure," the doctor told them. "And there appear to have been some changes in her genetic code. I don't know how this happened, and I can assure you that it's not serious as far as her general health goes, but . . ." He looked at Amy's mother helplessly, as if he didn't know the right words.

Ms. Candler spoke gently. "Everything that made

Amy exceptional, those genetic elements that gave her superior skills . . . they seem to have disappeared."

Tasha gasped. "You mean she won't get her powers back?"

"It doesn't look that way," Dr. Hopkins said. "Of course, given Amy's unusual makeup, we don't know anything for sure, but as of now, I can tell you that her genetic code is completely ordinary. Normal."

It took a moment for both Tasha and Eric to absorb this. Eric spoke first.

"But you said this isn't critical, right? She's going to be okay?"

"Well, in a sense, she'll be fine," the doctor said. "In the way that you and I and most people are fine. But she won't be like she was."

"But she won't die, or be sick anymore, right?" Eric pressed him.

"Right," Dr. Hopkins said. "She should remain in normal good health."

Eric sighed in relief. "Then it's not the end of the world."

But Tasha was thinking that to Amy it would be.

fourteen

Amy sat on the ledge of her bedroom window and watched Eric dribble a basketball on his driveway next door. Normally she would have gone outside and joined him. He always enjoyed the challenge of playing basketball with her, since she moved fast and her timing was perfect. Also, he loved seeing her make a basket every time. But that had been then; this was now. She wouldn't be shooting perfect hoops anymore.

Learning how to be a regular person sure wasn't going to be easy. Amy got off the ledge and went to her mirror. She still looked the same, of course—but she felt like a different person. With her back to the mirror, she pulled down the right sleeve of her T-shirt and looked over her shoulder at her reflection. The mark of the crescent moon—the mark that identified all the clones of Project Crescent—was still there. It hadn't faded, and it hadn't shrunk. It just didn't mean anything anymore.

She supposed she should get started on her homework. It was piled up on her desk. Normally she would never have considered doing homework on a Friday afternoon—she'd wait till Sunday night, knowing the homework wouldn't take up much of her time. But it might take a lot longer from now on.

Tasha had collected Amy's assignments from her teachers that afternoon. Dr. Hopkins had told Amy she could return to school, but she wasn't in the mood. She wasn't sure when or if she'd ever be in the mood. Of course, she'd have to go back to school eventually. It was more important now than ever, since she would have to learn everything the way ordinary people learned.

Moving restlessly around the bedroom, she looked for something to occupy her mind. Maybe a little rearranging would help. She'd been thinking of moving her desk closer to the window. Grabbing hold of one end of the desk, she pulled.

A week ago she could have lifted it easily. Now she

couldn't even drag it across the room. She should have known this would happen. A normal girl of twelve years old, who weighed no more than a hundred pounds, wouldn't be able to move a heavy mahogany desk.

But logic didn't matter. This was the straw that broke the camel's back. Amy sank down on her bed and burst into tears.

At that very moment Tasha came into the room. She hurried over to Amy, sat down, and put her arms around her.

"It's okay, it's okay," Amy said, wiping her eyes fiercely. "I'm just feeling a little frustrated, that's all. I'll get over it. I just have to get used to being . . ."

"Like the rest of us," Tasha finished, but there was no satisfaction in her voice. "You know what I think? I think you need to have some fun. Dr. Hopkins says you're perfectly healthy. Why don't you and Eric and I do something tonight?"

"Like rent a video and order a pizza?"

"No." Tasha shook her head. "You need to get out of the house. So do Eric and I. We've all been cooped up too long, worrying. We need to let off some steam."

Amy felt ashamed of herself. It had to have been pretty dreary for her best friend and her boyfriend. "Where do you want to go?"

"How about the Space? We could hang out, have a

raspberry soda, do some dancing. Your mother will feel a lot better if you go out too."

"Okay," Amy said, knowing her mother had worried enough lately. Besides, her bedroom was beginning to close in on her. "Let's do it."

"And dress up," Tasha ordered her. "We should look hot."

From the expression on Eric's face, Amy knew she had succeeded in following Tasha's orders. Her stretchy dress was perfect for dancing, and her strappy sandals gave her an additional two inches of height. She'd put her hair up for yet another inch. Tonight she needed all the confidence in the world.

"You look lovely, Amy," her mother said, not even commenting on the shortness of the dress.

"Thanks," Amy said. "Hey, Mom, now that my DNA is nothing special, can I get a professional haircut?" That had been a subject of debate for ages, since Nancy was always worried that Amy's hair would get into the wrong hands.

"I don't see why not," her mother said, clearly very relieved to see Amy dealing with the situation so well. She drove them over to Ace's Space and left them at the door.

The place was mobbed. Even though it had been

open less than a week, the Space had become hugely popular. With Eric and Tasha, Amy pushed her way through the crowd toward the bar. At one point, someone accidentally shoved her, and she bumped hard against a table. "Ow!"

"Are you okay?" Eric asked anxiously.

"Of course I'm okay," Amy said. "I'm not made of china, Eric." Still, she wondered if, for the first time in her life, she'd get a real, lasting black-and-blue mark.

It was a pain not having her super-vision. By the time she realized they were heading directly toward Jeanine Bryant and Linda Riviera, the two girls had both seen her. She knew they were probably talking about her, even though she couldn't hear them or see their lips well enough to read them. It was a real downer, knowing that Jeanine would have a much easier time now beating Amy at sports, getting better grades . . . Well, Amy was determined to exert herself like a normal person to excel.

"There's your pal," Tasha said to Eric as Ace Tolliver made his way through the crowd, shaking hands. Thinking about her silly suspicions and the way she'd tried to get into his office, Amy felt embarrassed as he approached them. But he gave no sign of holding anything against her. His smile actually broadened.

"Amy Candler, good to see you out and about," he declared. He slapped Eric on the back, said hello to Tasha, and moved on. Amy hoped Jeanine had seen this and wished she could watch her reaction. Jeanine would have to be impressed that Ace Tolliver knew Amy's name.

Someone pulled Tasha away to the dance floor, and Eric and Amy followed. The DJ was playing an old disco tune, and it felt good to Amy to release her tension by dancing. But it bothered her a little, the way Eric was moving protectively around her, trying to keep her from bumping into anyone. Just because she didn't have her powers didn't make her fragile. Was her new normal status going to make a difference in their relationship? She hadn't even thought about that yet. In fact, she hadn't thought about many things. And she didn't want to.

Right now, all that mattered was moving her body to the rhythm of the music. She'd always loved to dance and could keep going for hours. . . .

But not this time. Not anymore. After only thirty minutes, she was tired and out of breath. Eric could see this.

"Maybe we should sit down for a while," he said in

the protective voice that Amy was beginning to find annoying.

"I don't need to sit down," Amy snapped. "I'm just going upstairs to get some air. You stay here; I'll be right back."

But Tasha saw her move toward the stairs leading up to the lobby and came hurrying after her. "Are you feeling okay?"

Amy groaned. "Yes, I'm fine, it's just stuffy in here. For crying out loud, I'm not an invalid. I can still walk up stairs on my own." That didn't stop Tasha from following her to the lobby.

"We're just going out to get some air," Tasha told the bouncer as he opened the door. "I don't want him to charge us another entrance fee," she whispered to Amy.

Amy rolled her eyes. "I could have figured that out all by myself, Tasha. I may not have superior intellectual skills anymore, but I'm not an idiot."

"Okay, okay," Tasha said hastily. She gazed out at the street. "That's a police car over there."

"I'm not blind, either," Amy snapped. "There's no more super-vision, but I still have perfectly normal eyesight."

Now it was Tasha's turn to be exasperated. "I'm

not saying anything's wrong with your eyes. I'm just wondering what the police are doing here." Then she uttered a small moan. "Oh, no. Amy . . . do you think they're here because of that note I sent?"

Amy shrugged. "I guess it's possible. But don't worry, I won't tell anyone you're responsible." They went back inside.

"It's just us again," Tasha said to the bouncer. "We've already paid." But the bouncer wasn't listening. He was staring at the police car out front. Then he took his mobile phone and pressed some buttons.

Amy and Tasha started down to the Space. They practically collided with Ace Tolliver, who was running up the stairs.

"I'm going to get one of those yummy raspberry sodas," Tasha said to Amy. "You want something to drink?"

"No thanks," Amy said. "I'm going to find Eric. I want to show him I haven't fallen apart and I can still dance."

They separated, and as Amy walked through the crowd, it seemed that her eyesight was worse than she'd thought. People were looking a little blurry. She heaved a deep sigh. Was she about to go from being generally superior to being all-around inferior?

Then she sniffed. There was an odd smell in the air, something that hadn't been there before she went outside—something vaguely recognizable. But her thought patterns weren't as quick as they used to be.

Which was why she wasn't the first person to scream "Fire!"

fifteen

Amy could feel the heat; she could see the wisps of smoke rising in the air, and out of the corner of her eye, the flicker of a flame. It was horribly familiar, especially as the fear rose within her. But this was no dream. Screams of terror filled the room as the smoke thickened and enveloped them. Amy could hear voices yelling, "Don't panic, don't panic," but nobody listened. People were stampeding toward the stairs, and Amy was pulled along in the crush.

The smoke was heavier now, and it was getting harder to breathe. Screams were turning into gasping sobs. The heat from the fire seemed to be getting closer. And then Amy tripped.

It was impossible for her to fall, so many people were crushed together so tightly. But she looked down—and realized, to her horror, that what she had tripped on was a human being. "There's someone on the floor," she screamed, but her words were lost in the general shrieking that surrounded her. Somehow she managed to crouch down and got a grip on the person's arms. It was a guy. Amy didn't know him.

She'd had no idea a person could be this heavy. If only she could be her old self, if only her powers would return, she could easily carry this guy over one shoulder— but all she could do now was drag the inert form across the floor, trying hard to keep it from being trampled.

Once she got to the stairs, it was even more of a shock to realize that she didn't have enough strength to pull the guy up with her. Fortunately, someone behind her helped shove him up the stairs, and then he suddenly regained consciousness. Amy could feel him struggling to stand upright, and she was able to push him out into the lobby and to relative safety.

She didn't step out into the lobby herself. She knew

there had to be other people who'd been knocked down and trampled, who were lying unconscious on the floor of the basement. Shoving and pushing, she propelled herself back downstairs against the wave of people. Now the wail of sirens and the shattering of glass could be heard in the tumult. On the basement floor, flames were leaping higher, but the sound of water rushing through hoses told Amy that help had arrived.

But that didn't mean more help wasn't needed. She couldn't see anything, but, dropping to the floor, she began to crawl. She touched someone's hand and grabbed it.

And then someone grabbed her. "Come on, stand up, move!" an adult voice ordered her.

"There's someone lying here," Amy yelled back. "I have them in my grip!"

But whoever had taken hold of her was pulling her away. "No, no!" Amy screamed. "I want to help!"

"You can't help us, little girl!" the voice bellowed. "You're just in the way!" She felt herself being lifted, carried up a ladder, and shoved out one of the high windows that the firefighters had broken. Another pair of arms caught her.

"I'm okay! There are more people down there!"

she shouted as she struggled to free herself. But it was useless. She was an ordinary girl now, and there was no way she could break the hold of a strong firefighter.

She had never felt so powerless—and so utterly useless—in her life.

sixteen

The TV reporter on the Sunday noon news spoke solemnly. "Twenty-two teenagers remain in the hospital in serious condition," he intoned. "The majority suffer from smoke inhalation. Eight more are listed in critical condition with third-degree burns. While there have been no fatalities from Friday night's fire in Ace's Space, the teen club on Prince Street, doctors say that . . ."

Amy hit the Off button on the remote control and sank back on her pillow. No fatalities. Yet. But thirty people who could die. Every one of whom could have been saved if Amy Candler—Amy, Number Seven—hadn't lost her powers.

There was a light tap on her bedroom door. Amy said nothing, but her mother came in anyway. "How are you feeling?"

"Fine," Amy said automatically.

"Are you hungry? Do you want something to eat?"

"No. Thank you." Amy stared at the blank TV screen and waited for her mother to go away.

But Nancy didn't leave. She remained in the doorway, gazing at her daughter with compassion and concern. "You can't go on like this, Amy."

Amy picked at a loose thread on her bedspread. "Like what?" she asked dully.

"Honey, I know you're depressed. We all are. But you haven't left this room since Friday night. You haven't eaten, and Tasha says you're not sleeping. You're going to make yourself sick."

Sick! That was something else she'd have to adjust to—getting sick like other people. Somehow it didn't seem very important.

"This whole thing is awful," she said. "People are suffering. They might even die."

"I know," her mother said. "But you can't blame yourself. You did what you could."

"What I could," Amy echoed bitterly. "Which wasn't much."

"And that's not your fault! Amy, we may never know

what altered your genetic code, but it happened, and you're going to have to deal with it. You can't single-handedly stop a fire and save lives."

Amy knew that everything her mother said was true. It wasn't logical for her to blame herself for the tragedy. Just because she'd lost her powers didn't mean she'd lost her ability to think rationally. But that didn't make her feel any better.

"Mom . . . I just want to be alone for a while."

Her mother waited a few seconds, and then she nodded. After she had left, Amy got up to use the bathroom, but she stopped when she caught a glimpse of herself in the mirror.

She really looked awful. Her hair hung in unkempt clumps, and she was still wearing the clothes she'd had on Friday night. They smelled of smoke and perspiration.

Around her neck, the little silver crescent moon she always wore seemed to be mocking her, reminding her of what she used to be. Roughly she undid the chain and tossed it into a bureau drawer. The glitter in her earlobes reproached her too. How could she even think about jewelry when people might die because of her?

She was unscrewing one of the posts when Tasha came in. "What are you doing?"

Amy didn't reply, letting her actions speak for themselves. She pulled one earring out and went to work on the other.

"Amy, you can't take those studs out! Remember what Dr. Hopkins said? We have to leave them in for three weeks or the holes will close up!"

"Like I care," Amy muttered. She tossed the earrings into her bureau drawer.

"Well . . ." Tasha stood there looking helpless. "Have you seen Eric?"

"No."

"There's a woman downstairs who wants to talk to us. Actually, she's going around talking to everyone who was at the Space on Friday night. She's some kind of investigator, I think. Anyway, she needs to ask us questions about the fire."

"Tell her I don't feel like talking right now," Amy replied.

"Okay," Tasha said, and backed out.

Amy moved away from the mirror and threw herself down on her bed. She didn't want to talk, she didn't want to think. She wasn't even sure she wanted to live.

With a heavy heart, Tasha descended the stairs. She'd never seen Amy behave this way. The Friday-night tragedy was hitting them all very hard. When she closed her eyes, Tasha could still hear the screams, she could still see the fire and smell the smoke . . . but Amy was taking it the hardest.

The woman in the living room was refusing Nancy's offer of coffee or tea. Nancy looked at Tasha with a question in her eyes. Tasha shook her head.

"She doesn't want to talk about it."

"I can understand that," the woman said kindly. "Perhaps I can interview her later."

"I'll leave you two alone," Nancy murmured. With a glance toward the stairs, she went on to the kitchen.

"Tasha, let me explain who I am and why I'm here," the woman said. "I'm a representative from the insurance company that covered the building on Prince Street. Whenever something like this happens, we need to find out how and why. The police are investigating too. We all want to make sure it doesn't happen again."

Tasha shrugged. "It was a fire."

"Yes, we know that, but there are many ways a fire can start. There could have been faulty electrical wiring in the building. Or someone might simply have been careless with a cigarette."

"No way," Tasha replied. "I mean, I don't know anything about wiring. But no one was smoking in there. There's no smoking allowed."

"You don't think it's possible someone might have broken the rule?"

Tasha shook her head fervently. "No, the Space has a really strict policy about no alcohol, no drugs, no cigarettes."

"I see," the woman said thoughtfully.

"Those big bouncer guys are always roaming around and watching," Tasha went on. "If anyone breaks a rule, they're told to leave. No second chances."

The woman leaned forward and gazed at Tasha intently. "I want you to tell me everything you remember from the time you arrived at Ace's Space Friday. I know it's painful for you to recall that evening, but this could be very important."

She was right—this wasn't something Tasha wanted to remember. But she tried. "Well, we came in, and I talked to a couple of girls who are in my PE class. Then we danced for a little while. Then . . . then we got something to drink. Then I saw Amy, and we decided to go upstairs to get some air outside."

"Did you see anyone outside?"

"No."

"No one?" the woman pressed. "Nothing out of the ordinary?"

"No . . . well, there was a police car in front of the building."

"Before the fire?"

"Yes."

"What was a police car doing there?"

"I don't know," Tasha said. She felt a blush creeping up on her face.

The investigator gazed at her searchingly. "Are you sure? Are you sure you don't know something, Tasha?"

"Well, it's not relevant," Tasha said. "It doesn't have anything to do with the fire."

"Perhaps not," the woman said. "But I want you to tell me anyway."

It was so embarrassing. "You see, my friend upstairs, Amy, she was very ill last week. And she kept saying she thought she'd been given drugs at Ace's Space. It wasn't true; the doctor even tested her and there were no drugs in her system. But then she got a high fever, and she was talking crazy, and she made me promise I'd contact the police to tell them to watch Ace's Space. And I promised, and then I had to keep my promise." Tasha couldn't bring herself to look the woman in the eye. "It was all pretty stupid. When Amy got better, she couldn't believe she'd said those things, and I felt really dumb about sending the note. But maybe that's why the police car showed up."

The woman listened without comment or expression. But when Tasha had finished, she stood up. "Could

145

you come with me, Tasha? I'd like you to meet with my superior."

On Prince Street, police barricades had been set up in front of the burned building, but Eric found them easy to bypass. It made him feel sick to see the damage the fire had done, and when he thought about the people in the hospital, he felt even worse. He could only imagine what it was doing to Ace Tolliver.

The man had to be devastated. He'd planned a place where teens could hang out and be safe, a haven from school and home but without the dangers that could be lurking in the streets, even at the malls. Then this had to happen. Kids he'd wanted to protect were being hospitalized.

Eric wanted to see him, to express his sympathy, to show the tycoon some support. He'd been so kind to get that doctor for Amy. Now Eric wanted to be there for him. He supposed he could have called—but what he wanted to say would be said so much better in person.

Stepping over the shards of glass, he ducked under the plastic ribbon that had been strung across the shattered main door. The acrid smell inside brought back images of the fire. Shuddering, he hurried to the elevator and pressed the Up button.

Nothing happened, and he realized that the electricity was probably off. He found the stairs and began climbing.

He saw some damage in the stairwell, mainly dark stains on the walls, but it appeared that the fire hadn't ravaged the building. When he came out on the fifth floor, he could barely smell the smoke anymore.

"Mr. Tolliver?" he called. There was no answer, but the tycoon's office door was open. He went in to wait.

Eric wasn't a snoop, and he'd had no intention of sticking his nose in Mr. Tolliver's business, but the letterhead on the paper was so large he couldn't miss it: Arnold Vickers, M.D. And just under that, in all capital letters: RE: AMY CANDLER.

He couldn't resist the temptation of reading a letter with his girlfriend's name on it.

The message from the doctor was brief:

I've put her blood through every possible test and have to conclude that there is nothing unusual about this girl. She is completely normal. I see no reason why she would be trying to interfere with your plans.

Eric was puzzled. He'd expected the doctor to look for signs of illness in Amy, but the doctor's report confused him. Had Tolliver really been concerned that Amy might hinder the success of Ace's Space?

The telephone rang and Eric jumped. Then he picked it up. Before he could say anything, a guttural voice on the other end barked, "Tolliver?"

For some crazy reason Eric said, "Yeah."

"Heard about the fire," the voice said. "Someone got suspicious, huh?"

"Yeah," Eric said again.

"But you got rid of the stuff, right?"

"Yeah."

"Half a million up in smoke," the voice said in disgust. "Guess you didn't have any option. Are you going to reopen?"

"Yeah."

"So when do you want the next shipment delivered?"

"Shipment of what?" Eric asked.

There was a dead silence on the other end. Then a loud click as the connection was broken.

"Amy, I have to talk to you!"

"Not now, Tasha," Amy called out.

"Yes, now! You have to hear this!"

Amy had known her best friend long enough to know when she wouldn't give up. "Okay," she groaned.

Tasha came in and sat down on the bed. Her nose wrinkled. "You need a shower," she said.

Amy glared at her.

"Okay, okay," Tasha said hastily. "That's not important. But this is. That investigator I was talking to, she made me come to her office and talk to another investigator. And you're not going to believe what I found out. Remember those drug problems at Deep Valley and Plainview middle schools?"

Amy shrugged. "Yeah. Why?"

"Well, a lot of kids at Deep Valley hang out at Skate 'n' Bowl, that combination bowling alley and skating rink. And just across the street from Plainview is the Old-Time Soda Shoppe."

"So what?"

"They're both owned by Ace Tolliver. Just like the Space."

Amy stared at her. "So?"

"The investigator said the police have been trying to establish some connection between those places and the sudden appearance of drugs in the communities."

"They think Ace Tolliver has something to do with pushing drugs?" Amy asked in disbelief.

"There's no evidence," Tasha told her. "In fact, there's absolutely nothing to connect Tolliver with the drugs. But isn't it kind of interesting that he happens to own popular teen places in communities where there are drug problems?"

"It's just a coincidence," Amy said. "What does that

have to do with us, anyway? There weren't any drugs floating around at the Space."

"But you had feelings about that right from the start," Tasha pointed out. "A week ago you were saying you thought you'd been drugged by Ace Tolliver."

"I was having hallucinations," Amy reminded her. "There were no drugs in my system. I was just imagining things."

"Maybe," Tasha said. "And maybe not. You have all those powers, Amy, and they're not just physical. You can think faster too. Did it ever occur to you that maybe your instincts, your feelings, are sharper than other people's?"

"If they ever were, they're not anymore," Amy muttered. "Anyway, if the police suspect Tolliver of being involved with pushing drugs to teenagers, why don't they just go ahead and arrest him?"

"Because there isn't one teeny-tiny drop of evidence," Tasha said.

Amy looked up. Eric was standing in her doorway.

Tasha turned and saw him too. "Where have you been?" she asked.

Eric didn't say anything at first. It was then that Amy realized how ashen his complexion was.

"Eric?"

"I went to see Ace Tolliver," Eric told them. "And—

And . . ." He hesitated. "Amy, did you ever say anything to him about being, you know, different?"

"Don't be stupid," Tasha said. "Amy doesn't go around telling people she's a genetically designed clone."

But Amy was frowning. A tiny spark of memory was creeping across the edges of her mind. "When I climbed up his fire escape and he pulled me into his office, I might have said something . . ." Then, suddenly, like a flash of light, she had total recall. "I said, 'I'm Amy, Number Seven. I'm perfect. I'm stronger than you are!' " She looked at Eric. "Why are you asking me that?"

Eric bit his lip. "Um, it's a long story . . . anyway, while I was in Tolliver's office there was a phone call."

Amy listened to his report of the conversation, and then something very strange began to happen. Although she'd had no food and no sleep, her mind starting working rapidly. Of course, she could be jumping to crazy conclusions just because she was hungry and tired. But somehow she knew that wasn't the case.

"Eric, can you locate Tolliver?"

"I've got his mobile number," Eric replied.

"Do you think you could set up a meeting with him?"

"What are you talking about?" Tasha asked suspiciously.

"Evidence," Amy said. "Eric, call Tolliver. Tell him you have to see him today. I'm going to take a shower." She went to the door.

"Amy, what do you think you can do?" Tasha asked. Now she sounded frightened. "Remember, you're not the way you used to be."

"I know," Amy said quietly. "But I'm still a person. I'm a human being. And I have to do something."

seventeen

"But I don't understand," Tasha said as she wound the wire around Eric's bare chest. "How could kids be getting drugs from Tolliver? I mean, how do they know to go to him?"

"They don't," Amy replied, feeling a little better and a lot cleaner. "Now, I could be wrong, but it's starting to make sense. All these places he opens are designed to be popular with young teens, right? And all these places have refreshments, right? So I'll bet he puts small quantities of stuff into drinks, adding a little more every week until kids get addicted. Then he has people who work for him—like those bouncers, maybe—who go to the kids and offer more stuff at higher prices."

"But then everyone would get addicted," Eric said.

Amy shook her head. "Not necessarily. He's too smart to put his poison in everything. He probably chooses one item, like that creamy raspberry soda. Some kids don't like raspberry, or they drink the pineapple sodas or something else. So it's just an isolated group that gets hooked. But if it's a popular drink, it can be a big group."

Tasha blanched. "I was drinking those raspberry sodas! Am I hooked on drugs now?"

"I'm just using the raspberry soda as an example," Amy assured her. "The drugs could be in the root beer or the ginger ale. Besides, even if the drugs were in the raspberry sodas, you haven't had enough yet to get addicted. I'm sure he does this slowly so no one gets suspicious."

"How did you think of this?" Eric asked in admiration. "Ouch, that's too tight!"

"You don't want the wires to show through your shirt, do you?" Tasha retorted.

"Actually, you gave me the idea," Amy told Eric. "You said it was good business for Tolliver to make everything free on the opening night of the club. That way, kids would get hooked on the place and decide that it was worth paying for the next time. Well, it's the same thing. Kids are getting the drugs cheap, through the sodas. But when they're hooked, they have to pay a lot more."

"How come I didn't figure that out?" Eric wondered.

Amy grinned. "Because even without my powers I'm smarter than you are. Okay, let's test this thing. Eric, say something."

"Like what?"

Amy hit a button on the tape recorder that now rested on Eric's chest. *"Like what?"* they all heard. Eric then put on his shirt and buttoned it all the way up so nothing underneath showed.

"How did you know how to do this?" Tasha asked.

"TV," Amy said. "It's amazing what you can learn from cop shows. Tasha, get the binoculars from my desk drawer." Her head jerked up. "Who's that?"

"Who's what?" Eric asked.

"I heard someone outside." Amy went to the window and looked out. "Uh-oh, it's Dr. Hopkins. My mother probably called him to come look at me." Her brow furrowed. Then she brightened. "You know, this could work to our advantage."

Eric and Tasha followed her downstairs. "Hi, Mom, hi, Dr. Hopkins," she said cheerfully. Her mother looked at her in amazement.

"Amy? You're feeling better!"

"A little," Amy said. "We're going to the movies."

"That's a great idea," Nancy said enthusiastically. "I'll give you a ride."

"No, we want to walk," Amy said quickly. "But if I get tired, I might want you to pick us up." She frowned deeply. "Only I don't know what time the movie is over. Do you guys know?"

"No," Eric and Tasha said in unison.

"I guess I could call you from a pay phone," Amy told her mother. Then she frowned again. "But those pay phones are always broken, aren't they?"

"Yeah," Eric and Tasha chorused.

"Your mother's invited me to stay for dinner," Dr. Hopkins said. "Why don't you just take my mobile phone with you? Then you can call from anywhere."

Amy's eyes sparkled. "What a great idea! Thanks!"

Amazing how well her scheme was pulling together.

"Now, remember what you have to do," she said to Eric as they all walked to Prince Street. "Get him talking. Let him think you know something. Make it sound like you want to get in on the action—you know, like distribute drugs at school or something. As soon as he says something incriminating, make a sign. I know! Scratch your head. Tasha and I will be watching you through the binoculars. As soon as you scratch your head, we'll call the police."

They reached Prince Street and went to a leafy tree across the street from the Space. "Let me see the binoculars," Amy said to Tasha. She looked through the lenses and adjusted them. Then she took in her breath sharply. "He's already there; I can see him through the window. Okay, Eric, go. And don't forget to be standing in front of the window when you scratch your head!"

Eric took off in the direction of the building while Amy and Tasha crouched by the tree. "This is exciting," Tasha murmured.

Amy agreed. If this creep Tolliver was truly responsible for pushing drugs, not to mention the fire, he was going to pay. For the first time in a long while, she was feeling truly empowered.

Tasha reached out and took her hand. "You know what, Amy? Fancy genes or ordinary genes, you're still awesome."

"You too," Amy said. She glanced up at the fifth-floor window, without even remembering to use the binoculars. And this time she didn't need them. "Ooh, Eric's in the office!"

Tasha took the binoculars. "Yeah, I can see him!"

They both watched the window. Amy could see

Eric's mouth moving and Tolliver responding. Then Eric moved out of view.

"Stay by the window," Amy groaned, and fortunately, Eric remembered. But Tolliver had moved, so now she couldn't see him. It didn't matter—the signal would come from Eric.

She could feel her own heart pounding, and she could have sworn she could hear Tasha's. Then, at the same moment, both she and Tasha let out a little shriek. Eric was scratching his head.

Amy pulled the mobile phone from her pocket and punched in some numbers. "Hello, hello?" she cried. She looked at the phone. Then she hit the numbers again.

Tasha was still looking through the binoculars. "Amy, Tolliver's looking angry!"

Frantically Amy pressed buttons again. "Something's wrong! Maybe we're out of range!" She looked up. Now she couldn't see anyone in the window. "Tasha, come on!"

She raced across the street and into the building. She could hear Tasha behind her, but her friend was moving very slowly, especially considering the fact that her brother could be in serious danger. By the time Amy reached the fourth-floor landing, she couldn't even hear Tasha's footsteps, but she didn't wait for her to catch up. There was no telling what might be happening in Tolliver's office.

Amy dashed onto the fifth floor and figured out which office must be Tolliver's. She ran to the door and turned the knob.

It was locked.

She could hear something inside. It sounded like gasping. With all her might, she kicked at the door, and to her surprise, it burst open.

Ace Tolliver was kneeling on the floor, and Eric lay stretched out flat in front of him. Tolliver's hands were around Eric's neck.

Without hesitation, Amy leaped onto Tolliver's back.

Tolliver let out a yelp of surprise. Then he gave a scream of pain as Amy grabbed his ears and pulled.

Amy knew that having a hundred-pound kid on his back wouldn't overpower Tolliver. She expected him to toss her off with a shrug of his shoulders.

But he didn't. Or maybe he couldn't.

Amy released his ears, grabbed his arms, and yanked. He wasn't so tough. She was able to peel his hands from Eric's neck with just a little exertion. Then she heard Tasha behind her. "There's a phone on his desk—call the police!" Amy screamed. Meanwhile, Eric was pulling himself out from under Tolliver. He ripped off his shirt and tore the wires from his chest. Tolliver was struggling, but Amy held him still long enough for Eric to wind the wires around the tycoon's wrists and ankles.

"Police are on their way," Tasha announced, and sure enough, off in the distance, Amy could already hear the sirens. On the floor, Tolliver was staring up at Amy in a state of shock.

"How—How did you . . ." He couldn't even finish the question. Amy didn't know whether he was wondering how she'd figured out his scheme or how she'd over-powered him. In either case, she had the same answer.

"I'm not sure."

eighteen

A series of three chimes during second period on Monday indicated that an announcement would be coming over the intercom system.

"Amy Candler, Eric Morgan, Tasha Morgan, please report to Dr. Noble's office immediately."

Amy could feel the eyes of the class on her as she rose. Even the teacher was staring. Everyone had to be thinking she was in some kind of serious trouble to be called to the principal's office. She wasn't too sure herself what to expect.

When she arrived at Dr. Noble's office, Eric and Tasha were already there. So were two police officers.

And Dr. Noble was looking particularly stern, though Amy could have sworn she detected a glint in the principal's eyes.

"I should be scolding the three of you," Dr. Noble said. "And of course, I will have to consider a long stretch of detention. You have taken major risks which were way beyond your capabilities, and you could have suffered dire consequences."

She let those words sink in while the three of them squirmed in their seats. Amy didn't think there was any point in attempting to justify their actions. She was already in serious trouble at home. Her mother had not been happy when the police brought the three of them back from Prince Street, and she had assured Tasha and Eric that their parents would not be pleased when they heard what their kids had done. It was quite possible that they'd all be grounded for the rest of their lives.

"On the other hand," Dr. Noble continued, "according to these police officers, you three have somehow managed to put a major drug dealer out of work. And for the lives you may have saved, well, some leniency is in order."

One officer spoke. "Tolliver was a real piece of work," she said. "He came across as super-clean, like an honest-to-goodness philanthropist. No one really knew how he'd made his fortune. There isn't that much money in providing dancing and bowling hangouts for teens. Everyone thought he was doing good things for young people. But it turns out that his real income came from the exploitation of kids. He created addictions in innocent victims and then used his so-called bouncers to follow up on the kids and offer to sell them stronger stuff."

The other officer said, "He made such a big deal about the fact that his places were squeaky clean that no one really suspected him. He put up a great front."

"No kidding," Eric said feelingly. "I thought he was such a neat guy."

The first police officer continued. "When he saw one of our cars in front of the Space on Friday night, he panicked. His first big shipment had come in that morning, and the stuff was being introduced into drinks for the first time that evening. He thought we had somehow been alerted to this, so he destroyed the evidence by setting the fire."

"Only the fire didn't finish the job," the second officer told them. "We've analyzed drinks, and we've got the chemical evidence."

"Not to mention what he said on your tape," the first officer told Eric. "That should give us enough to put him away for a long, long time."

Eric beamed. But he wouldn't take all the credit. "It was Amy who first thought Tolliver was a sleazebag," he declared proudly.

"Just a feeling I had," Amy said vaguely.

"She gets very strong feelings," Tasha piped up.

"Well, that's interesting," the policewoman said. "It's good to have sharp instincts. But what I can't understand is how you overpowered him."

"We did it together," Amy said quickly.

"But according to what Tasha and Eric have told us, you were the one who was able to stop Tolliver from strangling Eric. How did you do that?"

Amy pretended to hazard a guess. "Maybe I just took him by surprise. I don't know."

But she did know. It was all coming together. The way she'd figured out Tolliver's scheme so quickly. Seeing into the fifth-floor window without any binoculars. Racing up the five flights of stairs in the Prince Street building. And, of course, overcoming the man himself.

Her powers were coming back.

It made no sense to her; she didn't know what was happening, and she didn't dare hope that she would again be the perfect person she once had been. But a little more speed, a little more strength, a little sharper vision were enough to be grateful for. She didn't need to know why she had them.

But that very afternoon, she found out.

Dr. Hopkins appeared at their house, and he looked almost as disheveled and sleep-deprived as the driven young scientist of twelve years earlier that Nancy Candler had described. When Amy answered the door, he staggered into the living room with an ecstatic expression.

"David!" Nancy cried in alarm. "What happened to you?"

"I figured it out!" he cried joyfully. "I know what happened to Amy! And it was all my fault!"

"Well, don't keep us in suspense," Nancy said. "What did you learn?"

"It's her earlobes!" Dr. Hopkins exclaimed. "You see, I'm not a very good housekeeper." He paused to catch his breath, and Amy was now thinking that perhaps he had gone off the deep end.

"I don't clean up very well," he said. "And in my office, I found a bit of cotton I'd used to swab Amy's earlobes when I pierced them. I analyzed the blood on the cotton. Amy . . . your earlobes are your Achilles' heel!"

Amy blinked. "Huh?"

"Amy!" Tasha said. "Don't you know the story of Achilles in Greek mythology? When he was born, he was dipped in some magic water that made him invulnerable. No one could ever hurt him. But he was held by one heel when he was dipped, so that part of his body was never submerged. That heel wasn't protected! That's how he was killed. Someone shot an arrow into his weak heel!"

"Wait a minute," Eric said. "Are you saying that one of those Crescent scientists held Amy by her earlobes?"

"No, no," Dr. Hopkins said. *"Achilles' heel* is just an expression. In the genetic design of the Amys, somehow or other the earlobe was excluded. Or maybe that part of the Amy structure had some sort of quirky response to the genetic manipulation. In any case, the piercing of the earlobe put Amy's entire DNA into a kind of short circuit, disrupting her entire cellular makeup. And her genetic code immediately deteriorated until it was no better than an ordinary human being's!"

Nancy took in her breath. "Ohmigod, David. What does this mean?"

"I don't know," he said, his dark-circled eyes bright with anticipation. "But this is giving me some very thrilling material to work with! And I'm getting back into clone research!" He and Nancy began talking science-speak about future research at a rapid and excited rate. But Amy wanted some immediate information.

"What about me?" she demanded. "Am I going to be like I used to be?"

Dr. Hopkins examined her earlobes. "The holes are closing," he said. "There's a strong possibility that once they completely heal, you will have all your former powers."

"Yay!" Amy squealed. "No offense, guys, but I really didn't like being normal."

"But now you won't be able to wear real pierced earrings," Tasha said mournfully.

"I know," Amy said. "And that's too bad. But it's not the end of the world."

When Amy went down to dinner that evening, Tasha and Eric had secret smiles on their faces. Earlier, they had taken off on a mysterious mission, and they now presented Amy with a small, handsomely ribboned box.

"What's this?" Amy asked, but they just grinned as she untied the ribbon and opened the gift.

"Oh, you guys," she moaned happily.

Nestling in thick cotton were dozens of earrings—sparkling gems, glittery studs, hearts and flowers, and more. But they were all the kind that could be stuck onto the earlobes. They were made for someone who could never again pierce her ears.

And all Amy wanted at that moment was enough strength in her arms to hug both Tasha and Eric at the same time.

Don't miss

replica

#10
Ice Cold

Amy's secret is out! Her worst enemy, Jeanine, knows that Amy is a clone. Now Amy fears the worst. She's sure Jeanine will blab the truth to everyone—maybe even try to sell Amy's story to some sleazy tabloid. But Jeanine never gets a chance to make good on any of her threats.

An accident leaves her in a coma.

Rumors of foul play spread like wildfire.

The number one suspect . . . Amy.

Sure, Amy wanted to stop Jeanine's big mouth, but maybe she wasn't the only one. . . .